PAPER STORIES

by Jean Stangl

Fearon Teacher Aids

a division of

David S. Lake Publishers

Belmont, California

Editorial director: Ina Tabibian
Editor: Robin Kelly
Designer and illustrator: Walt Shelly
Cover designer: Walt Shelly
Production editor: Anne Lewis

ISBN–0–8224–5402–5

Library of Congress Catalog Card Number: 84-60238

Printed in the United States of America.

1. 9 8 7 6 5 4 3

Contents

*These stories have paper-cutting activities that are appropriate for children to do.

*These stories have paper-cutting activities that are appropriate for children to do.

Introduction

Making paper cutouts while telling a story is an old Chinese art. In fact, the concept of accompanying stories with a paper-cutting activity may have been a forerunner to shadow puppet plays, which originated probably in China and were popular throughout many cultures. Hans Christian Andersen was famous for his paper cutouts. He created and used cutouts as visual aids while telling the fairy tales for which he was so well-known. Many of his paper sculptures are on display at the Hans Christian Andersen Museum in Odense, Denmark.

In this book, 31 stories are presented for storytelling to young children. Preschoolers through third graders will enjoy hearing these fun, easy-to-tell stories. Some stories relay factual information of interest to children who are curious about how trees grow or how snowflakes form. A few stories reinforce basic concepts (such as shape recognition and counting) that are critical to early learning. Other stories encourage listener participation by asking questions for the group to answer.

Teachers, librarians, parents, and caregivers will find that children are fascinated with this unique approach to storytelling. Paper cutouts accompanying the stories will aid in lengthening a child's attention span and provide a visual reinforcement for the story. Older children will enjoy reading the stories and making their own cutouts to use as tangible props in retelling the stories.

Every story includes a paper-cutting activity for the storyteller to perform while relaying the story to a group of children. Materials and any preparation required before the story begins are listed above the story title. Simple directions for folding, cutting, and presenting the paper cutouts are given within the story. Each paper cutout that you produce will complement and enhance the story told.

All patterns for the paper stories are reproducible, and most stories call for 8½″ × 11″ paper. You may wish to reproduce the pattern, then cut and fold the copied pattern. Instead, you may wish to trace the cutting and folding lines from the reproducible patterns onto another sheet of paper. An easy method of transferring the lines is to place the pattern over a sheet of construction paper, keeping the sheets of paper together. Using a writing instrument or a thumbnail, press firmly over the cutting and folding lines on the pattern. This will produce an indentation representing the lines from the pattern onto the construction paper, and your cutout will be free of distracting drawn lines.

Several reproducible patterns have simple enough folding and cutting designs that the children themselves could make the cutouts while an adult or an older child reads the story and directs the cutting activity. These nine stories are indicated by asterisks in the table of contents. Choose carefully: young children usually have difficulty cutting curved lines. Some patterns are easy to cut, but directing the cutting may be a little difficult. Blunt-end scissors are sufficient for the paper cutting of most stories. However, sharp-tipped scissors will help in the paper cutting for "Joey Finds a Friend" and "Two Scared Mice."

Before presenting a story to a group of children, you may wish to read the story once or twice. It helps to become familiar with the story so you can concentrate on doing the paper cutting, creating a theatrical presentation, and developing rapport with your listeners during the storytelling. You may also wish to make sample cutouts beforehand. With a little practice, any storyteller will soon become adept at presenting paper-cutting stories.

Part 1
HOLIDAYS

For this story you will need an 8½" × 11" piece of orange construction paper and a pair of scissors. Trace the folding and cutting lines from the pattern. Follow the directions for cutting the paper.

The Little Orange House

Once upon a time a very small witch was walking in the woods. The cold wind was blowing the dry leaves all around her. The little witch was frantically searching for a house for the winter. She could not find one. Suddenly a piece of orange paper, blown by the wind, landed at her feet. She picked it up.

The little witch looked closely at the paper and then she said, "I shall make myself a little house from this piece of orange paper."

She folded the paper in half. Then she took her scissors (she always carried a pair in her pocket) and she cut off the two corners to make a roof. It looked like this.

"This will do just fine," she said as she looked at her new house. "But I will need a door." With her scissors she cut a door. Since witches always wear pointed hats, she cut a special door. It looked like this.

The little witch walked through the door into the little orange house. It was very dark inside. She quickly hurried back out.

"I will need to make windows to let in the light," said the little witch. She cut a front and back window that looked like this.

Oh, it was a very fine-looking house. Her very own little house with a roof, a door, and windows was all finished. But just as the little witch started to go inside for the winter, she saw a tiny ghost floating down the windswept path. As the tiny ghost came to a stop near the little house, the little witch saw that the ghost was crying.

"Why are you crying?" asked the little witch.

The tiny ghost stopped crying and answered, "It is cold and windy. It is getting dark, and I have no place to spend the winter."

"You may spend the winter with me in my new house," said the kind little witch.

"Oh, thank you," the happy tiny ghost said as she peeked in through the window. "This is a very nice house."

"First," said the little witch, "I will need to make you a little door of your very own." She took her scissors again and began to cut. She cut a very tiny door. It looked like this.

The two happy new friends went inside. The tiny ghost went in the very little door, and the little witch went through her own special door. All winter long they lived happily together inside the little orange house.

If you want to see inside their little orange house, just unfold the sheet of paper. Surprise!

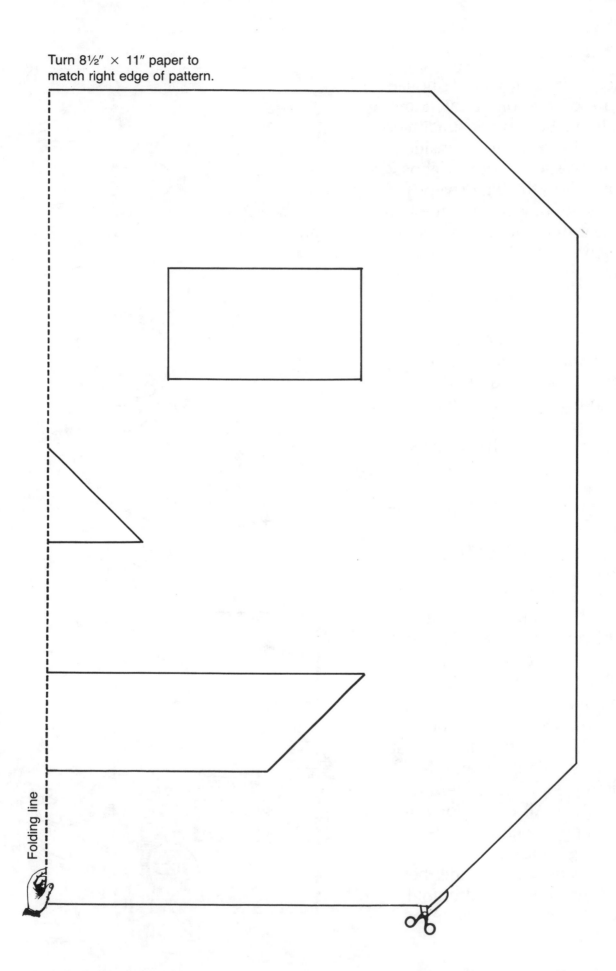

Turn 8½″ × 11″ paper to
match right edge of pattern.

Folding line

A Special Thanksgiving Table

You will need scissors and one 8½" × 11" sheet of paper. Trace the cutting and folding lines from the pattern.

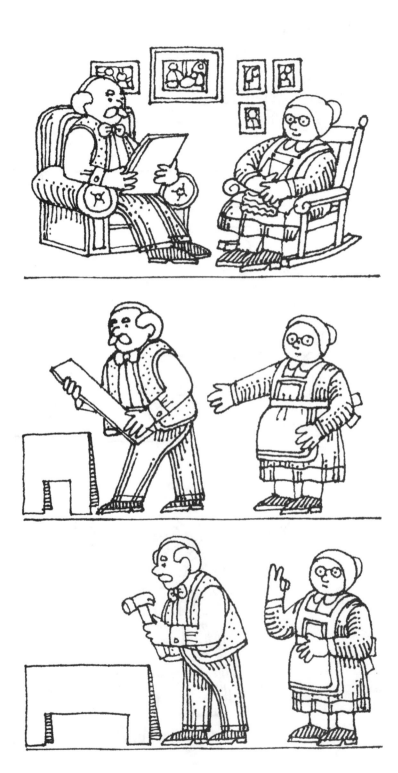

Grandma and Grandpa needed a new table for their Thanksgiving dinner.

"This year there will be only the two of us for dinner," said Grandma.

"I will make us a small table," said Grandpa. He went out to his workshop. Grandpa found a board that was just the right size. (*Cut the paper around line 1 and discard the outer portion. Fold on line 2.*) Grandpa took out his hammer and saw. (*Fold on line 3.*) He worked and worked. (*Fold on line 4.*) Soon he had a table that was just right for two people. (*Cut out A.*)

Grandma opened the door and called, "Our son and his wife are coming to dinner. We will need a bigger table."

"I will make the table bigger, then," said Grandpa. He hammered and sawed. (*Cut off left legs of table from portion A to line 4.*) He measured and nailed, and he had a table this size. (*Unfold line 4.*)

The next day, Grandma told Grandpa, "My two sisters are coming for Thanksgiving dinner too."

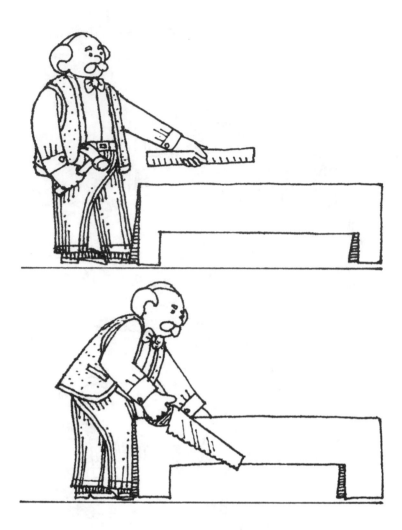

Grandpa said, "Then I will make a bigger table." He cut and sawed. (*Cut off left legs of table to fold line 3.*) He measured and he nailed until he had a very big table. (*Unfold line 3.*) It looked like this.

That afternoon, Grandma said, "I am sorry dear, but we will need an even bigger table. Our grandchildren are coming for dinner too."

"Yes, I will have to make a bigger table," said Grandpa. He decided that he would make a special place for all the grandchildren. (*Refold line 3.*) He sawed and sawed and sawed. (*Cut out B and unfold 3.*) "There," said Grandpa, "my grandchildren will sit here in the center."

"Grandpa," called Grandma, "your cousins called, and I invited them to dinner. I also got a letter from your brothers, and they are coming too. We will have to have a bigger table."

"I can't make a bigger table," said Grandpa. "I have no more wood and no more nails."

"Oh, what will we do?" wondered Grandma. "It is Thanksgiving. We must have a table big enough for all of our family."

"I will see what I can do," said Grandpa. He thought and he thought. Suddenly Grandpa had an idea. (*Fold on line 5.*) He could solve the problem quickly. (*Refold on line 3.*) He took his saw, and he made one last cut. (*Cut out C.*) He trimmed the legs a wee bit. (***Trim all legs about ⅛″.***) "Come and see!" he called to Grandma. "Now there will be room for everyone." (***Unfold line 3 and separate to show two tables.***)

"And room for turkey and pumpkin pie and cranberries and. . . ." interrupted Grandma. (***The group can name additional foods.***) "Grandpa, you are the very best table maker!" she said.

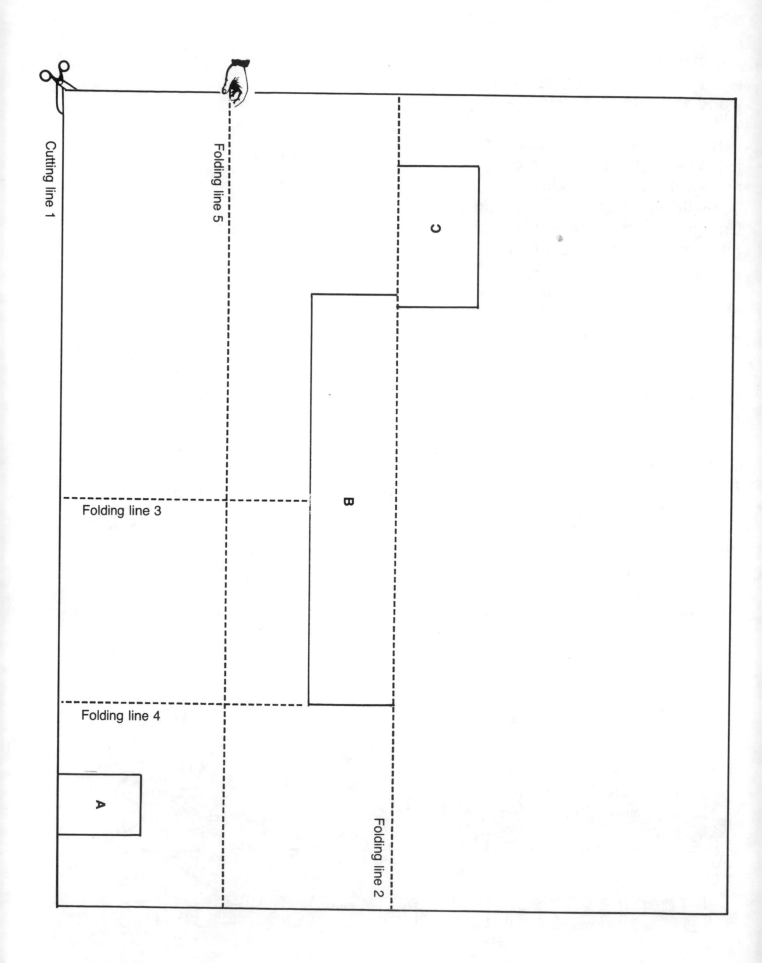

Morris Mouse and His Christmas Trees

You will need one 8½″ × 11″ sheet of green construction paper and scissors. Fold the paper on the folding line, and trace the cutting lines from the pattern.

One cold winter night, Morris Mouse crawled up out of his mouse hole. He set out to find a Christmas tree for his family. Deep in the forest, Morris discovered a beautiful tree. It had a good trunk (*cut from 1 to 2*), a nice shape (*cut from 2 to 3*), and it came to a point at the top. (*Cut from 3 to 4.*) Morris used his sharp teeth and gnawed away at the trunk. Nibble, nibble, nibble. The tree fell to the ground. (*Unfold.*) He dragged the tree back to his house. The little mouse tried to get the tree into the long hole that led to his house.

"This tree is much too big," said Morris, and off he went to look for a smaller tree. (*Refold the paper.*) "There is the perfect tree," he thought. It, too, had a good trunk (*cut from 5 to 6 to 7*), a nice shape (*cut from 7 to 8*), and came to a point at the top.

(*Cut from 8 to 9.*) Nibble, nibble, nibble, went Morris, and the tree tumbled down. (*Unfold.*) He pulled it back to his house and tried to get it into his mouse hole.

"This tree is still too big," said Morris, and off he went to look for a smaller tree. (*Refold the paper.*) There by the pond stood a smaller tree. "Looks good," said Morris. It had a good trunk (*cut third tree the same as the other trees*), a nice shape, and came to a point at the top. Morris sawed through it with his sharp teeth. Nibble, nibble, nibble. Down fell the tree. (*Unfold paper.*) The mouse carried it back home and tried to get it into his mouse hole.

"This tree is too big too!" Morris said. Off he went to look for a smaller tree. (*Refold paper.*) Near the road, he saw an even smaller tree. It had a good trunk (*cut fourth tree the same as other trees*), a nice shape, and it came to a point at the top. Nibble, nibble, nibble. Down came the tree, and Morris hurried back to his house. (*Unfold paper.*) He couldn't get this one into the hole either.

"Even this little tree is too big," said Morris, and he went off again to find a tree. (*Refold the paper.*) Then he saw a very tiny tree. It had a good trunk (*cut fifth tree the same as other trees*), a nice shape, and came to a point at the top. Quickly he chewed through the trunk. Nibble, nibble, nibble. Down it fell. (*Unfold paper.*) Morris picked up the tree and ran all the way home.

"This tree is just the right size," he said. But just as he started down his mouse hole, he saw the four other trees lying in the snow. Morris had an idea!

He took the biggest tree over to Dolly Deer's house and left it by her door. (*Open first tree.*)

He took the next biggest tree over to Frankie Fox's house and left it by his door. (*Open second tree.*)

He took the medium-sized tree over to Ruthie Rabbit's house and left it by her door. (*Open third tree.*)

He took the last tree over to Charlie Chipmunk's house and left it by his door. (*Open fourth tree.*)

Morris smiled as he carried the tiny tree into his mouse house to surprise Mrs. Mouse and all the little mice. (*Show fifth tree.*)

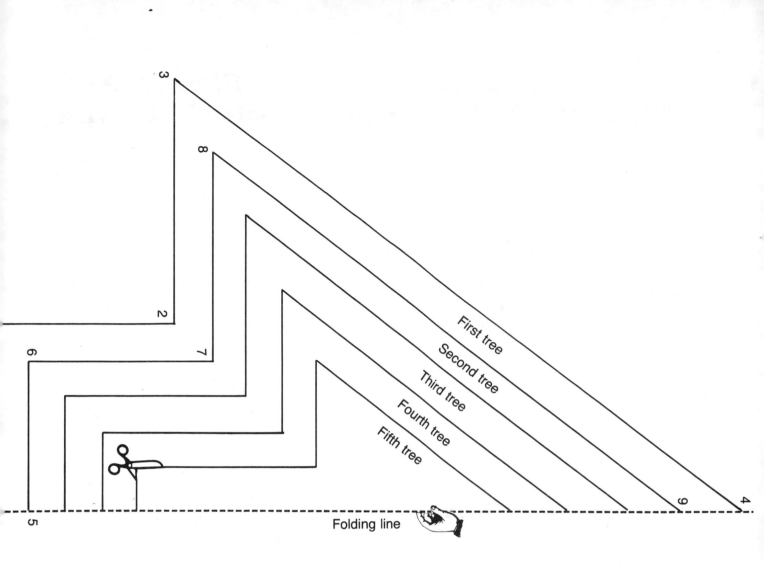

3

8

2

6

7

First tree

Second tree

Third tree

Fourth tree

Fifth tree

9

4

5

Folding line

You will need one 8½″ × 11″ sheet of green construction paper and scissors. Fold the paper on the folding line and transfer the cutting lines from the pattern.

Pine Tree's Great Surprise

Deep in the forest grew a pine tree that wanted to be a Christmas tree. During the summer storms, it had been hit by lightning (*cut from 1 to 2*), burned on one side (*cut from 2 to 3*), and had its top broken off. (*Cut from 3 to 4.*) It didn't look at all like a Christmas tree. And it was winter now.

Pine Tree was feeling very sad. Just then, Gray Squirrel came bouncing through the forest. He saw Pine Tree.

"What is the matter?" asked Gray Squirrel.

"I will never be a Christmas tree now," said Pine Tree. "I have no place for hanging a star, no pretty branches for ornaments, and no trunk under which to place gifts.

They will probably cut me down for firewood."

"That makes me feel sad too," said Gray Squirrel, "but I must be getting home." He scampered off into the woods.

That night, Gray Squirrel called his friends Blue Jay, White Rabbit, Brown Beaver, and Red Deer to his house. "Pine Tree is afraid of being cut for firewood and is feeling very sad," said Gray Squirrel. "We must do something to help him."

"I will help," said Blue Jay.

"Me too," said White Rabbit.

"I am a good helper," said Brown Beaver.

"But what can we do?" asked Red Deer.

All night the animals thought and thought. Finally they had a plan. Early the next morning, while it was still dark, the animal friends went to the place where Pine Tree grew. Pine Tree was fast asleep. Quietly the friends started to work.

Blue Jay flew to the top of the tree and pecked away. Peck (*cut from 4 to 5*), peck. (*Cut from 5 to 6.*)

Red Deer bit into the tall branches. Bite (*cut from 6 to 7*), bite (*cut from 7 to 8*), bite. (*Cut from 8 to 9.*)

Brown Beaver chewed in and out along the side. Chew (*cut from 9 to 10*), chew (*cut from 10 to 11*), chew. (*Cut from 11 to 12.*)

Gray Squirrel stuffed branches into the empty spaces. Stuff (*cut from 12 to 13*), stuff (*cut from 13 to 14*), stuff. (*Cut from 14 to 15.*)

White Rabbit nibbled at the bottom of the tree. Nibble (*cut from 15 to 16*), nibble. (*Cut from 16 to 17.*)

The animals were finished. They waited quietly by the tree. Soon the sun shone softly on the tree. Pine Tree woke up and saw his shadow. (*Unfold paper.*)

"Look at me! I am beautiful," said Pine Tree.

The animals smiled. "Tomorrow we shall decorate you and make you our own special Christmas tree," they said.

"Thank you, animal friends," said the tree. "Now I shall never be cut for firewood."

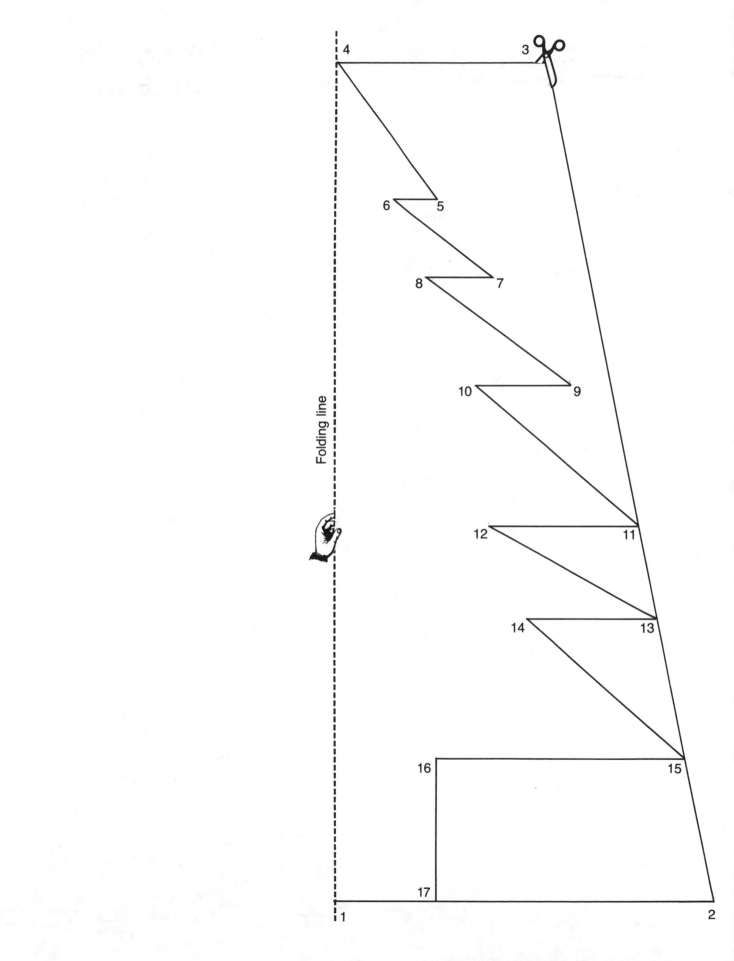

Cut a 27″ × 4″ strip from a lightweight brown paper bag or from newspaper. Fold the strip into accordion pleats, making 1½″ folds. From the pattern, mark the points for cutting. Hold the paper strip by the edge having only folds.

Who's in the Barn?

A jolly, fat man walked up a long, snowy path. (*Cut from point 1 to 2.*) At the end of the path, he jumped over a big rock. (***Don't cut between 2 and 3.***) Quickly he walked back a few short steps. (*Cut from 3 to 4.*) Up and over a small drift of sparkling snow he climbed. (*Cut from 4 to 5 to 6.*) Next, he trudged up to the end of a long row of sweet-smelling pine trees. (*Cut from 6 to 7.*) Around the trees and down the other side he went. (*Cut from 7 to 8.*) After a few hurried steps, he stood beside his trusty sled. (*Cut from 8 to 9.*) He checked it out, turned, and slid down the steep hill. (*Cut from 9 to 10.*) Then the little man, who had a fluffy white beard, walked straight into the barn. (*Cut from 10 to 11.*)

Who do you think was in the barn? (*Cut from 11 to 12. Unfold the pleats, one at a time, and call out each of the following names: Dasher, Dancer, Prancer, Vixen, Comet, Cupid, Donner, Blitzen, and Rudolph.*)

(*Let the group guess who the little man is.*)

Folds

8 7

10

9 5

12 11 6

4 3

2

1

Outer edges and folds

You will need scissors and one 8½″ × 11″ sheet of red paper. Trace the cutting lines from the pattern.

A Valentine for Kitten

It was February 14th. This was the day that Kitten was coming to live at the farm. The barnyard animals were eating their breakfast.

Horse said, "We must make something to give Kitten for a welcome gift."

"What could we make?" asked Goat.

"It has to be something special," said Pig.

"We could give her this pretty piece of red paper." said Duck.

"Let me see that," said Horse. She took the piece of paper, folded it like this (*fold paper on the folding line*), and began to nibble around it. (*Cut on line A.*) "How is this?" (*Unfold.*)

"No," said Goat, "it is too big. Let me try." (*Refold.*) Goat munched all around the paper. (*Cut on line B.*) "How is this?" he asked. (*Unfold.*)

"No," said Pig. "It is still too big." (*Refold.*) Pig chomped all around the paper. (*Cut on line C.*) "How is this?" he asked. (*Unfold.*)

"No, it's not quite right," said Duck. (*Refold.*) Duck pecked all around the paper. (*Cut on line D.*) "Is this all right?" (*Unfold.*) Duck looked at the shape and thought about it a minute before deciding to try one more time. (*Refold and cut on line E.*)

"How is this?" asked Duck. (*Unfold.*)

"It is just the right size," said Horse.

"Perfect," said Pig.

"Wonderful," said Goat.

"Quiet," said Duck, "here she comes."

Slowly, Kitten walked into the barn.

"Hello! Welcome to the farm," said the animals as they gave the valentine to Kitten. (*Hold up fifth heart.*)

"Thank you," she said happily. Then Kitten looked down at the barn floor and saw all the scraps of red paper. She picked them up, one at a time, and said, "Here is a valentine for you, Duck." (*Hold up fourth heart.*) "Here is a valentine for you, Pig." (*Hold up third heart.*) "Here is a valentine for you, Goat." (*Hold up second heart.*) "And here is a valentine for you, Horse." (*Hold up first heart.*)

It was indeed a happy day when Kitten came to the farm.

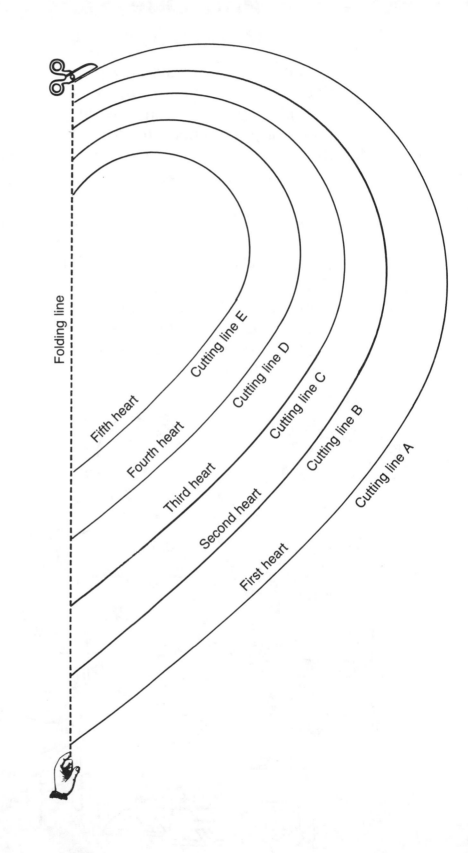

Folding line

Fifth heart

Fourth heart

Cutting line E

Third heart

Cutting line D

Second heart

Cutting line C

Cutting line B

First heart

Cutting line A

Six Little Girls and One Valentine

You will need one 8½″ × 11″ sheet of pink paper and scissors. Trace the folding and cutting lines from the pattern.

Once there were six little girls. Each little girl wanted to make a valentine. But they had only one piece of pink paper. They tried to think of a way to make six valentines. They looked at the paper. They folded the paper once. (*Fold on line A.*) They folded it twice. (*Fold on line B with portion 1 under portion 2.*) They folded it a third time. (*Fold on line C with portion 3 behind 2.*) Finally, they decided to fold it one more time. (*Fold on line D through all thicknesses of paper.*)

The first little girl said, "I'll cut here," and she did. (*Cut from 1 to 2.*)

The second little girl said, "I'll cut here," and she did. (*Cut from 2 to 3.*)

The third little girl said, "I'll cut here," and she did. (*Don't cut from 3 to 4; cut from 4 to 5.*)

The fourth little girl said, "I'll cut here," and she did. (*Cut from 5 to 6.*)

The fifth little girl said, "I'll cut here," and she did. (*Don't cut from 6 to 7; cut from 7 to 8 to 9.*)

The sixth little girl said, "Let's go play," and they did. (*Keep paper folded.*)

They left the folded pink paper on the table. Suddenly, the wind came through an open window and blew the paper onto the floor, right where the six little girls were playing.

The first little girl said, "I see one pretty valentine." (*Unfold line D to show one valentine heart.*)

And the wind blew.

The second little girl said, "I see two pretty valentines." (*Unfold line C, showing two valentine hearts.*)

And the wind blew.

The third little girl said, "I see three pretty valentines." (*Unfold line B to show three valentine hearts.*)

The wind stopped blowing.

The fourth little girl said, "I don't see four."

The fifth little girl said, "I wish there were five."

And the wind blew and blew and blew.

The sixth little girl said, "Look, I see six!" (*Unfold line A and count hearts 1 to 6.*) There were six pretty valentines for six pretty girls.

Turn 8½″ × 11″ paper to
match right edge of pattern.

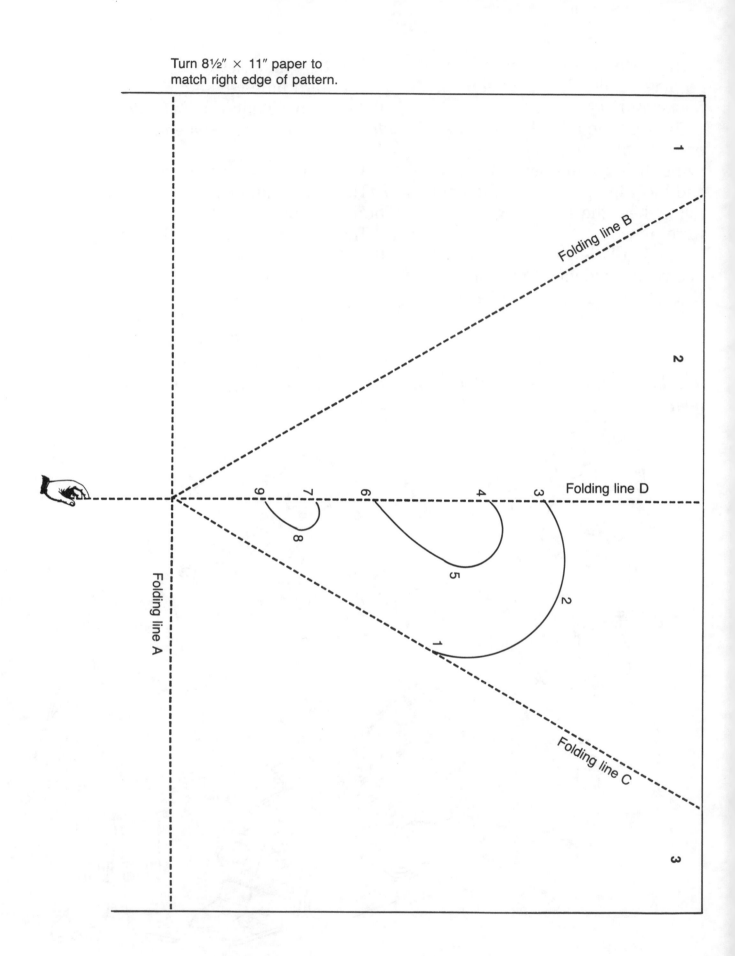

1

Folding line B

2

Folding line D

Folding line A

Folding line C

9 7 6 4 3

8

5

2

1

3

The Wind and the Red Paper Square

Once there was a red paper square that had been dropped into the river. The square did not wish to be carried out to sea. But having no way of getting out of the river, the red paper square decided to call upon the wind.

"Wind, wind, please blow me out of this river before I get too soggy."

The wind answered by blowing the red paper square out of the river and onto the grassy bank.

As the red square lay on the bank drying out, he complained to the wind, "I am tired of being a square. All I have are four straight sides and four sharp corners. I wish I could be a different shape."

"Well," the wind said, "perhaps I can use my special powers to make you into another shape."

"Oh, thank you," said the red square. "You are a good friend."

So the wind gave a big puff and blew off one side of the red square. (*Cut along line A.*) Now it looked like this.

"I do look different," said the red paper, "but this is not a good shape for me. Wind, wind," he called, "use your special powers to make me into a different shape."

The wind gave another big puff and blew the red paper in half from one corner to the other. (*Cut along line B.*)

"Yes, this is a nice shape," said the red paper, "but it still is not quite right for me. Wind, wind, use your special powers to make me into another shape."

The wind thought that the red paper was hard to please, but it decided to try again anyway. This time the wind gave three short puffs and blew off each corner of the red paper. (*Cut along lines C, D, and E.*)

"This is indeed an unusual shape," said the red paper. "Still, I don't think this is a good shape for me. Wind, wind, use your special powers and try one more time to change me into the right shape."

The wind was tired, but it agreed to try one more time. Gathering up all its special powers, the mighty wind blew one side of the red paper over on top of the other side. (*Fold line F.*) Then the wind nipped at the top and slashed at the bottom of the red paper. (*Cut on line G through both sides of the folded paper.*)

Because the wind was tired of trying to please, it blew the red paper high into the air. Over the rooftops the paper floated. Finally it came to rest in the middle of a sidewalk. Just then, a little girl walked by. She picked up the red paper and unfolded it.

"Oh, look," said the little girl, " someone has sent me a pretty red . . ." (*Unfold the paper as the group says the shape.*)

Begin with a square shape.

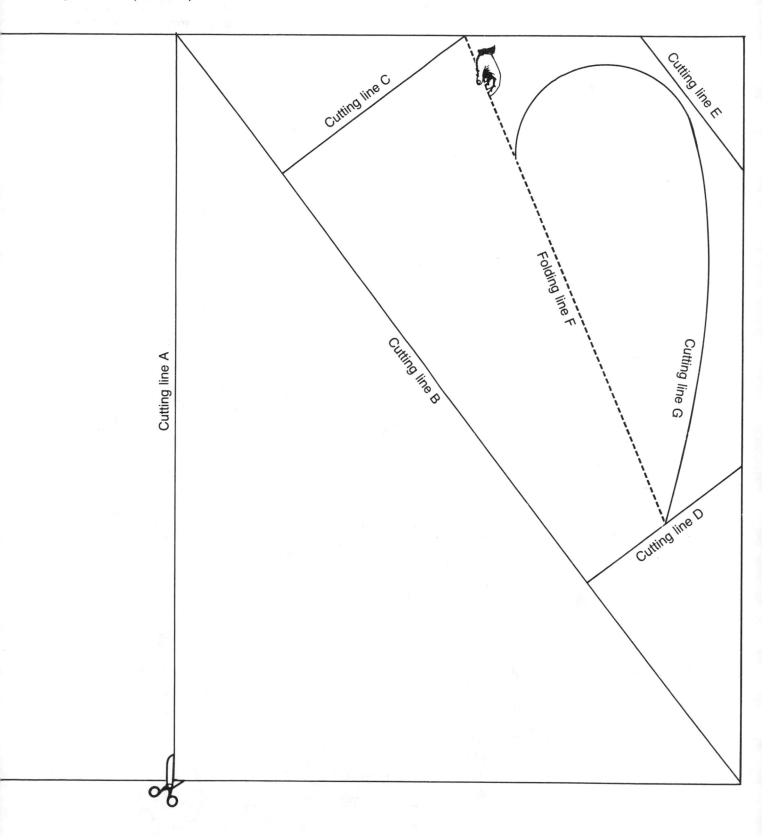

The Chocolate Easter Egg

For this story, you will need scissors and two sheets of 8½" × 11" paper, one white and one brown. Fold both sheets along the folding line. Place white sheet inside brown. Trace cutting lines on paper according to the pattern.

One day a little boy was walking in the woods. He heard a noise.

"Who is there?" he called. But no one answered. He ran all around the woods looking for someone or something. (*Begin slowly cutting on the outside line.*)

"Where are you?" he asked. But still there was no answer. He looked up high. He searched through the trees. He looked underneath the logs, but he could not find anything. The little boy ran up to the end of the path. On top of a flat rock, he found (*unfold, showing only the brown side*) a big chocolate Easter egg.

On the egg, there was a note that read, "If you want to find out who left this egg, follow these directions." (*Fold the egg again along the folding line.*)

The little boy carefully followed the directions that told him to do these things:

He ran around the big lake. (*Cut from 1 to 2.*)

He pushed through the bushes. (*Cut from 2 to 3.*)

He climbed over a rock. (*Cut from 3 to 4.*)

Then he tripped and tumbled down a hill. (*Cut from 4 to 5.*)

He waded across a stream. (*Cut from 5 to 6.*)

Up a small hill. (*Cut from 6 to 7.*)

Into a valley. (*Cut from 7 to 8.*)

Slowly he made his way to the top of the mountain. (*Cut from 8 to 9.*)

He slipped and slid down the other side. (*Cut from 9 to 10.*)

He was so tired. The little boy took one more step and sat down to rest in the shade of a big tree. (*Cut from 10 to 11.*)

He heard the noise again. He wiped his eyes and looked up. There stood (*unfold to show the white side*) the Easter Rabbit! Behind him stood another rabbit! (*Show both rabbits.*)

Before the little boy could say anything, both rabbits hopped off into the woods. (*Rabbits disappear behind you.*)

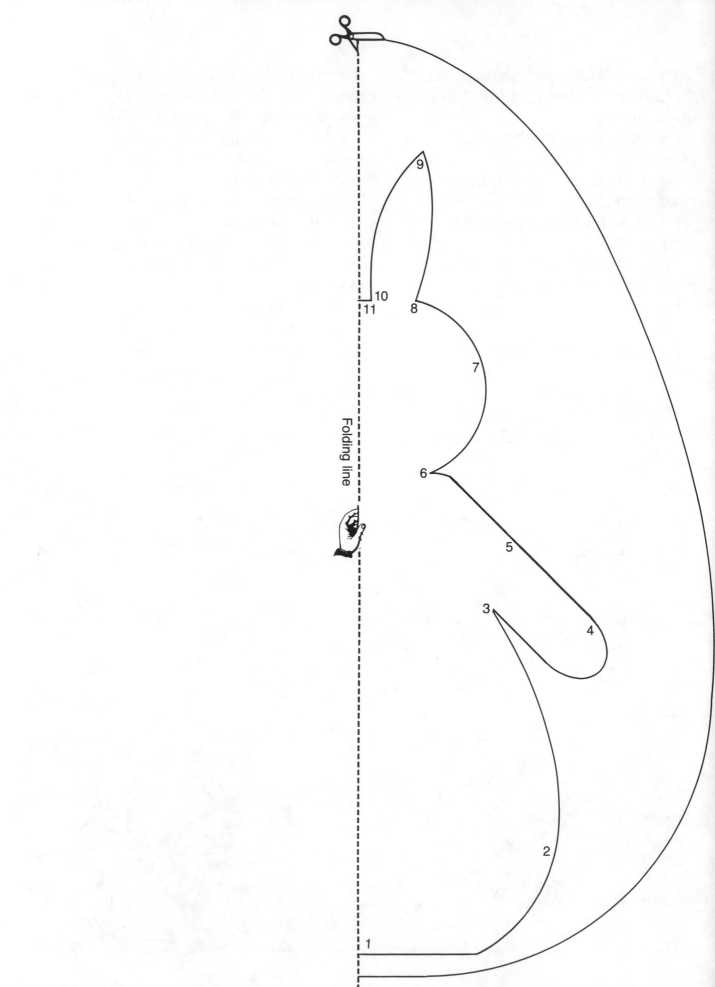

Folding line

Lost and Found

You will need scissors and one 5½" × 10½" sheet of white paper. Fold the paper into six 1¾" accordion pleats. Trace the cutting line from the pattern.

The Rabbit family was on its way home when they decided to cut through Mr. Green's vegetable farm and have their supper. Everyone was busy nibbling the crisp, fresh vegetables.

After a short while, Mrs. Rabbit looked around for her children and asked, "Where did they go?"

"We must have lost them," said Mr. Rabbit.

Frantically, Mr. and Mrs. Rabbit began searching. They hopped down through the rows of carrots. (*Cut from 1 to 2.*)

"Not here," said Mr. Rabbit.

They leaped over the log at the end of the field. (***Don't cut between 2 and 3.***)

Up through the rows of lettuce went the mother and father rabbits. (*Cut from 3 to 4.*)

Mrs. Rabbit called, "They're not here either."

In and out of the broccoli beds they ran. (*Cut from 4 to 5.*)

"We must find them," said Mr. Rabbit.

Hop, hop they went, up the hill where the celery grew. (*Cut from 5 to 6.*)

"Nothing here," said Mr. Rabbit.

Down the side of the cabbage field hopped the worried Mr. and Mrs. Rabbit. It was almost dark when they stopped to rest. What could have happened to the children!

Suddenly, they saw something move. (*Cut from 6 to 7 to 8.*)

There, asleep under a giant cabbage plant, were (*unfold*) three baby rabbits. Mr. and Mrs. Rabbit had found them at last.

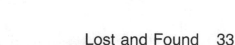

Folds

Outer edges and folds

6

7

8

5

4

3

2

1

Part 2

NATURE

Caught in the Storm

For this story you will need a pair of scissors and a piece of white paper, 5″ × 6″. Fold the paper to make it 5″ × 3″. From the pattern, mark the points for cutting. Hold the paper on the fold.

Deep in the forest, on a soft mound of snow, sat a shivering little rabbit. The snow was piling up and the wind blew circles of snow all around him. The little rabbit was cold, and he was lost. He stood up tall on his hind legs and sniffed the air. He had to find a safe place to spend the night.

Suddenly he knew where he would be warm. The rabbit began to run through the snow as fast as he could. Soon he found a place that was just right for him. (*Cut from 1 to 2 to 3.*) The rabbit crawled under it, snuggled down, and went to sleep.

Soon a bushy-tailed squirrel came scampering along. He too was looking for a place to spend the night. The squirrel saw where the rabbit had gone. He found a place there for himself. (*Cut from 3 to 4 to 5.*) He curled his tail around himself and went to sleep.

Next, a little bird with white-tipped wings fluttered down to the ground. She was looking for shelter from the cold, cold wind. She saw where the other animals were hiding and joined them. (*Cut from 5 to 6 to 7.*) The little bird tucked her beak under her feathers and went to sleep.

The three animals didn't see something else that was hiding in the safe place they'd found. It was an owl with big, round eyes. The owl was waiting for night. She closed her eyes, gave a soft "hoot," and went back to sleep. (*Cut from 7 to 8 to 9.*) It was just too cold to go hunting.

By now, night had come. The snow had stopped falling and the moon had begun to shine. The four sleeping animals were snug and warm throughout the long, cold night. The animals had found shelter (*cut from 9 to 10*) under a tree like this one. (*Unfold the paper.*)

Folding line

8
9
6
7
4
5
2
3
1
10

The Disappearing Snowperson

You will need scissors and one 8½" × 11" sheet of white paper. Fold the paper on the folding line. Trace the cutting lines from the pattern.

On Monday, I made a snowperson.
(Cut on line A.)

Just like that!
(Unfold paper.)

On Tuesday, the wind blew some snow away.
(Refold; cut on line B and discard outer portion.)

Just like that!
(Unfold paper.)

On Wednesday, it rained on my snowperson.
(Refold; cut on line C and discard outer portion.)

Just like that!
(Unfold paper.)

On Thursday, the hot sun started to melt it.
(Refold; cut on line D and discard outer portion.)

Just like that!
(Unfold paper.)

On Friday, it melted into a puddle.
(Refold; cut on line E and keep only the oval shape.)

Just like that!
(Unfold paper.)

On Saturday, it snowed again.
Just like that!
On Sunday, I made another snowperson.
(Cut on line F.)

Just like that!
(Unfold paper to show little snowperson.)

MONDAY

THURSDAY

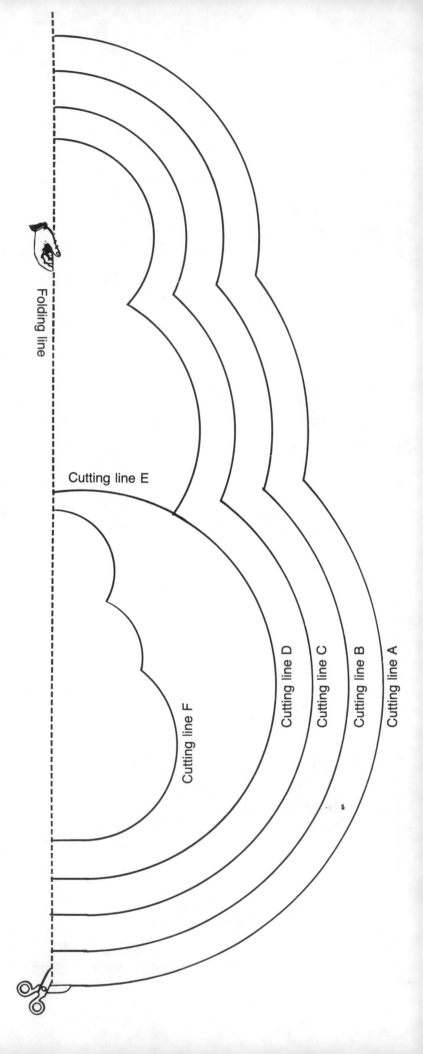

Folding line

Cutting line E

Cutting line F

Cutting line D

Cutting line C

Cutting line B

Cutting line A

The Happy Raindrop

You will need scissors and one 8½″ × 11″ sheet of white paper. Fold on line A. Trace the other folding and cutting lines from the pattern.

Drip Drop was a little drop of water that lived high up in a cloud. Many other drops lived there too. (*Fold on line B.*)

They had been raindrops millions of times before. Sometimes they would end up in puddles, lakes, rivers, or maybe in the ocean. (*Fold on line C.*) When the moist air became warm, the water drops were pulled up toward the sky. Many, many water drops would group together then and make a cloud.

The water drops stayed with Grandfather Cloud while they waited for the air to cool. Then they would become raindrops, fall from the cloud, and water the dry earth. It happened over and over again. (*Fold on line D.*)

One day Drip Drop said, "I don't want to be a raindrop next time. I want to be a snowflake and parachute down to earth."

"Whoever heard of such a thing?" said one drop.

"How can that be?" asked another drop.

"We have always liked being raindrops," said a third drop. (*Cut from 1 to 2.*)

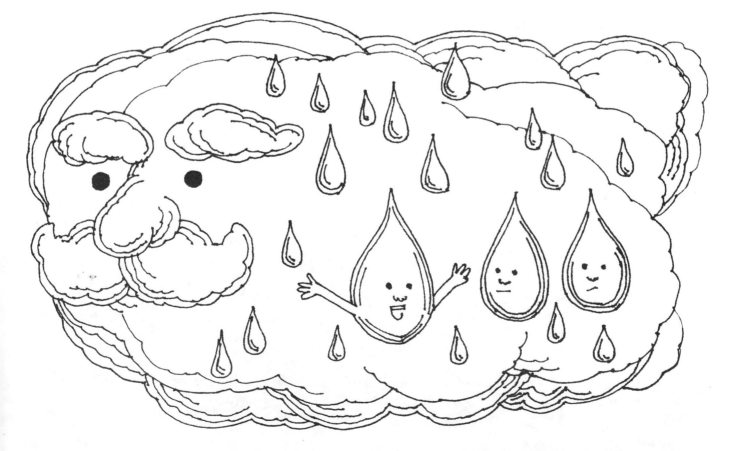

"I will talk to Grandfather Cloud," said Drip Drop. "He will know how to help me."

"Grandfather Cloud," he said to the wise old cloud. "The next time I fall, I want to be a snowflake."

Grandfather Cloud thought for a moment and then said, "Well, I don't know about that, but I will see what I can do." (*Cut from 2 to 3.*)

Many weeks passed. The wind carried the cloud far away. The water drops stayed in the cloud. (*Cut from 3 to 4.*)

The cloud moved into a very cold region. The water droplets were freezing. They were stuck to tiny pieces of dust from the cloud, and they turned into ice crystals. Drip Drop was so heavy that he began to fall through the cloud. He bumped into other ice crystals, and he stuck to some of them. (*Cut out 5 and 6.*)

Drip Drop grew larger and heavier. "I'm cold. I'm freezing," he said. Suddenly he fell completely out of the cloud. (*Cut out 7 and 8.*)

"What is happening to me?" he wondered. "I feel different." He looked around and saw many beautiful, tiny glistening objects in the sky. Each was a different shape, but each one had six sides. (*Cut out 9 and 10.*)

Down, down floated Drip Drop. He was parachuting down to the earth. "This is fun!" he thought. Then he fell softly on top of a big pile of snow. Drip Drop was happy because now he was a (*unfold*) snowflake.

Turn 8½" × 11" paper to
match right edge of pattern.

This cutting pattern is given as a guide. The
six-sided figure can be cut freehand if you
wish.

Folding line B

Folding line D

Folding line A

Folding line C

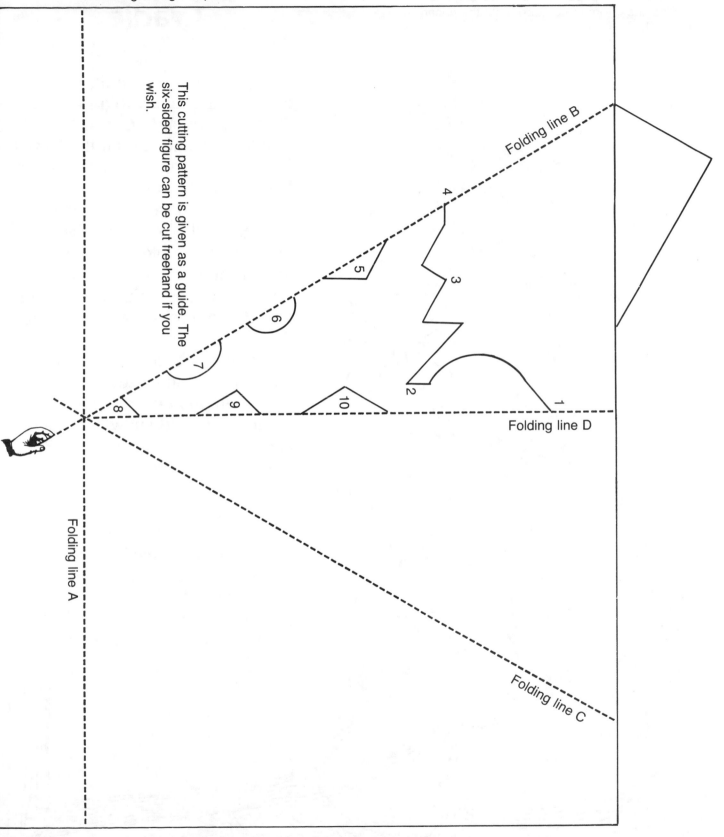

You will need scissors and one 8½″ × 11″ sheet of brown paper. Trace the folding and cutting lines from the pattern. Fold the paper on the folding line.

The Little Brown Cradle

High up in a tree, a little brown cradle clung tightly to a branch. (*Cut on lines A, B, C, and D.*)

Autumn came and all the leaves fell from the tree. The little brown cradle was the only thing left on the tree. Wind said, "I am very strong. I will blow down the cradle." The wind blew hard and tore at the edges of the cradle. Whooo. Whooo. (*Cut from points 1 to 2 and 5 to 6.*) But the cradle did not fall.

Winter came. Snow said, "I will cover it over and freeze it." Snowflakes fell and covered the brown cradle. The cold snow froze here and it froze there. (*Cut from 2 to 3 and 6 to 7.*) Brrr. Brrr. But when the snow melted, the brown cradle was still there.

Spring came. Rain said, "I will wash it away." Huge drops of rain fell on the little cradle. Drip. Drip. (*Cut from 3 to 4 to 9 and from 7 to 8 to 9.*) Down came the heavy rains. But the brown cradle hung on tight.

Hail said, "I will beat down on it, and surely it will fall." Large hailstones fell and made several holes in the cradle. There was one hole here and another one there. (*Cut out the two areas marked by Xs.*) Ping. Ping. But even hail couldn't knock down the cradle.

Sun said, "I will shine my brightest. It will be so warm that the cradle will have to let go." The hot rays of the sun shone brightly. (*Cut out two areas marked by Ys.*) The brown cradle got warmer and warmer. The sun was very hot. (*Cut out other two areas marked by Ys.*) The brown cradle got so warm that it split open. (*Unfold paper slightly.*) Out flew a beautiful brown (*unfold*) moth.

When summer comes, the moth will fly away and lay an egg for another brown cradle.

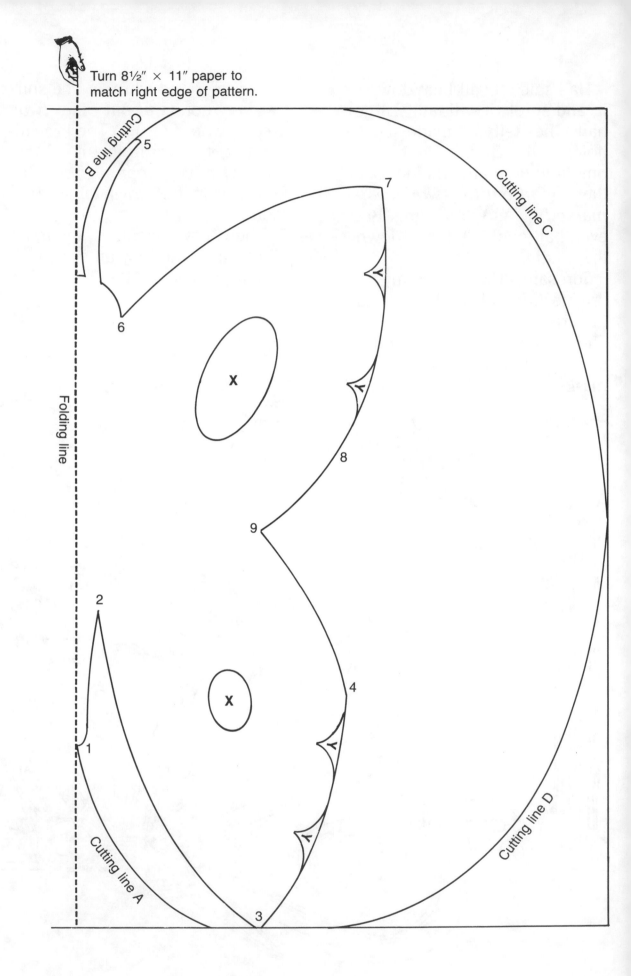

Turn 8½″ × 11″ paper to match right edge of pattern.

Cutting line B

Folding line

Cutting line C

Cutting line A

Cutting line D

5

6

7

8

9

X

X

2

1

4

3

What Am I?

You will need scissors and one 8½″ × 11″ sheet of yellow paper. Trace the folding and cutting lines from the pattern.

I hide all day.
(Fold the paper on the folding line.)
At night I play.
(Cut from point 1 to 2.)
I am one in a million.
(Cut from 2 to 3.)
It could be a billion.
(Cut from 3 to 4.)
I give off light.
(Cut from 4 to 5.)
And I shine at night.
(Cut from 5 to 6.)
I'm a *(unfold paper)* star!

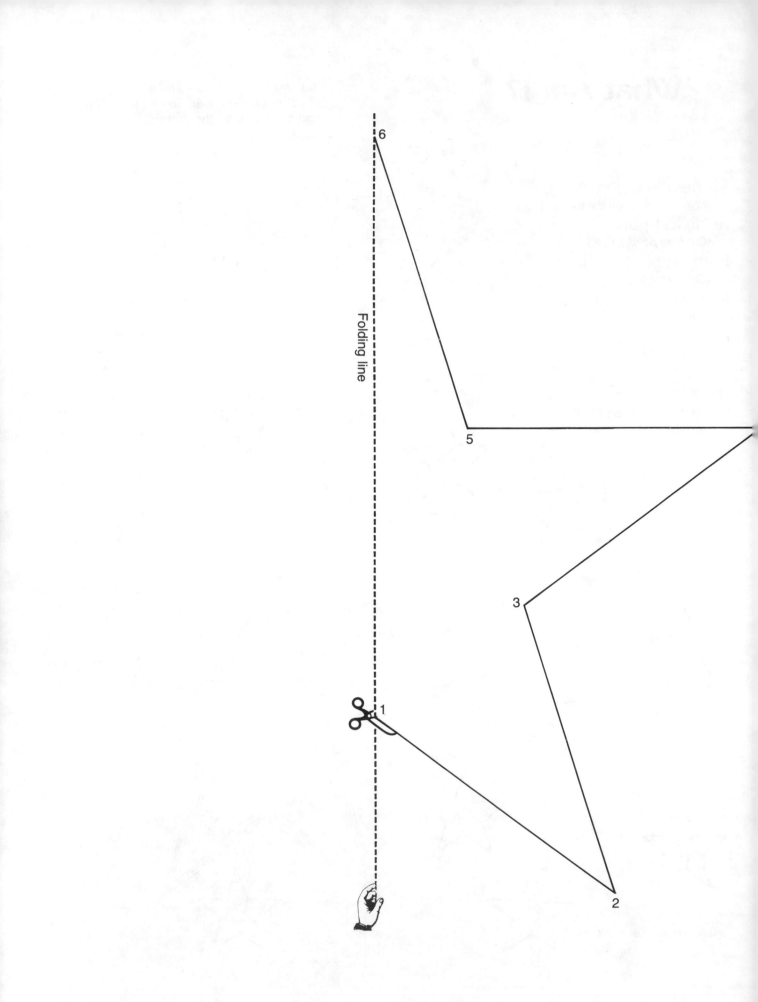

Folding line

Part 3

RHYMES
AND
CONCEPTS

You will need scissors and one 5″ × 18″ piece of white shelf paper. Fold the paper into 10 accordion pleats, each 1¾″ wide. Trace the cutting line from the pattern.

Five Little Snowboys

Once upon a time, a little girl made a big, big snowball. Next, she made a middle-sized one. Then she made a tiny one. She put the snowballs one on top of the other. On the very top, she put a hat.

"I will make a snowboy," the little girl said. "Scoop, scoop. Pat, pat. Scoop, pat, pat." (*Cut on the solid line. **Don't cut on the folds.** Then unfold the paper as you say the rhyme.*)

She made one little snowboy.
  He fell and bumped his head.
  (*Unfold one snowboy.*)

She made two little snowboys.
  They went riding on a sled.
  (*Unfold another snowboy.*)

She made three little snowboys.
  They marched off to bed.
  (*Unfold third snowboy.*)

She made four little snowboys.
  They wore ties of red.
  (*Unfold fourth snowboy.*)

She made five little snowboys.
  And she named them each Ted.
  (*Unfold last snowboy.*)

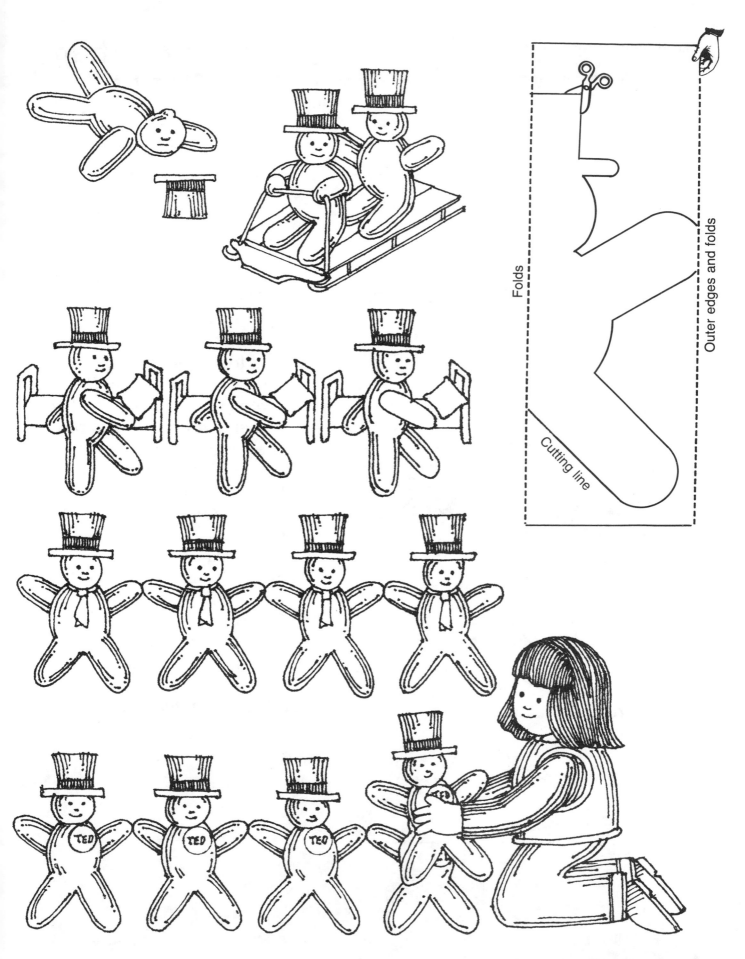

Folds

Outer edges and folds

Cutting line

Five Little Snowboys   51

You will need scissors, a hole punch, and one 8½″ × 11″ sheet of paper. Trace the folding and cutting lines from the pattern. Fold the paper on the folding line.

The Funny-Shape Family

The Shape family works at the circus. They perform tricks for everyone to see. Right now, it is time for them to perform.

Father Square comes on stage first.

(Cut on lines A, B, C, and D. Then cut to the edge of the paper.)

Big Brother Rectangle stands next to Father Square.

(Cut on lines E and F. Cut along line G from line F to H; then cut on line H to the edge of the paper.)

Mother Circle stands next to Big Brother Rectangle. We can see only half of her because she is carrying Little Baby Circle.

(Punch out X.)

Sister Triangle stands next to Mother Circle and Little Baby Circle.

(Cut on line I.)

How many members of the Shape family can you find? (*Cut on line J and unfold.*)

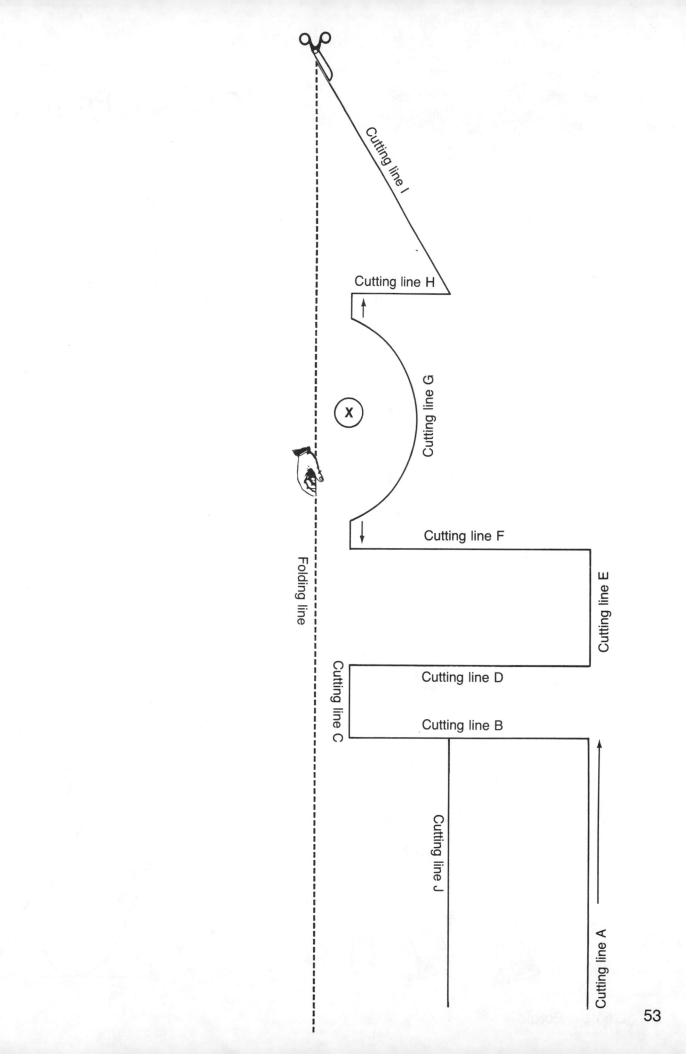

Cutting line I

Cutting line H

Cutting line G

X

Folding line

Cutting line F

Cutting line E

Cutting line D

Cutting line C

Cutting line B

Cutting line J

Cutting line A

You will need scissors, one 4½″ × 10½″ strip of white paper, and one 4½″ × 3½″ piece of green paper. Place the green paper on top of the white strip with right edges meeting. Accordion pleat the paper together into 1¾″ folds. Trace the cutting lines from the pattern.

Georgie Porgie

Georgie Porgie
   (*cut along line A*),
pudding and pie
   (*cut on line B; don't cut the folds*),
Kissed the girls and made them cry.
   (*Unfold, but keep green cutout hidden.*)
When the boys came out to play
   (*refold paper and cut along lines C and D; unfold*),
Georgie Porgie ran away.
   (*Separate the green boy and pull it away.*)

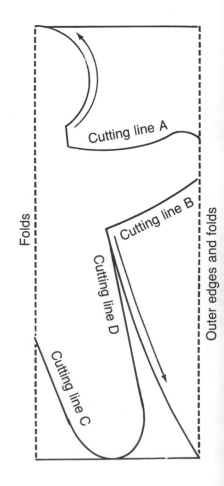

Folds

Cutting line A

Cutting line B

Cutting line D

Cutting line C

Outer edges and folds

Hickety Pickety

You will need one twelve-section egg carton, scissors, and two 3″ × 10½″ pieces of white tissue paper. Place one piece on top of the other and fold them together into 7/8″ accordion pleats. Trace the cutting line.

Hickety Pickety, my fat hen
   (*cut on line 1*),
She lays eggs for gentlemen
   (*cut on line 2; don't cut the folds*),
Sometimes five (*slowly unfold paper*),
and sometimes ten
   (*unfold and separate the two sheets*),
Hickety Pickety, my fat hen.
That doesn't look right. Maybe I
should count again.
   (*Refold paper.*)
Sometimes six (*slowly unfold paper*),
and sometimes a dozen
   (*unfold and separate the two sheets*),
Hickety Pickety, my fat hen.
   (*Cut the eggs apart and drop one into each
section of the egg carton to show that 12
equals one dozen.*)

Both pieces of 3″ × 10½″
tissue paper folded together.

Cutting line A

Folded edges

Outer edges and folds

Cutting line B

7/8″ folds

You will need scissors and one 8½″ × 11″ sheet of orange paper. Trace the folding and cutting lines from the pattern. Fold the paper along the folding line.

Little Bug, Little Bug

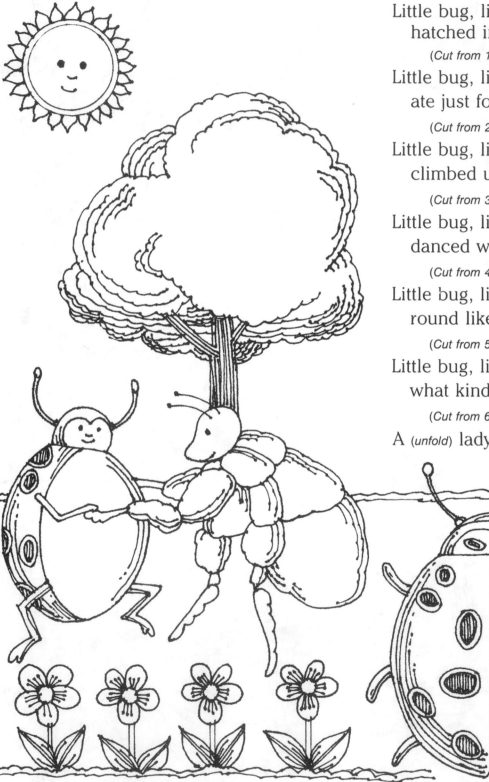

Little bug, little bug,
hatched in the sun.
    (Cut from 1 to 2 along line.)

Little bug, little bug,
ate just for fun.
    (Cut from 2 to 3.)

Little bug, little bug,
climbed up a tree.
    (Cut from 3 to 4.)

Little bug, little bug,
danced with a flea.
    (Cut from 4 to 5.)

Little bug, little bug,
round like a pie.
    (Cut from 5 to 6.)

Little bug, little bug,
what kind am I?
    (Cut from 6 to 7.)

A *(unfold)* ladybug!

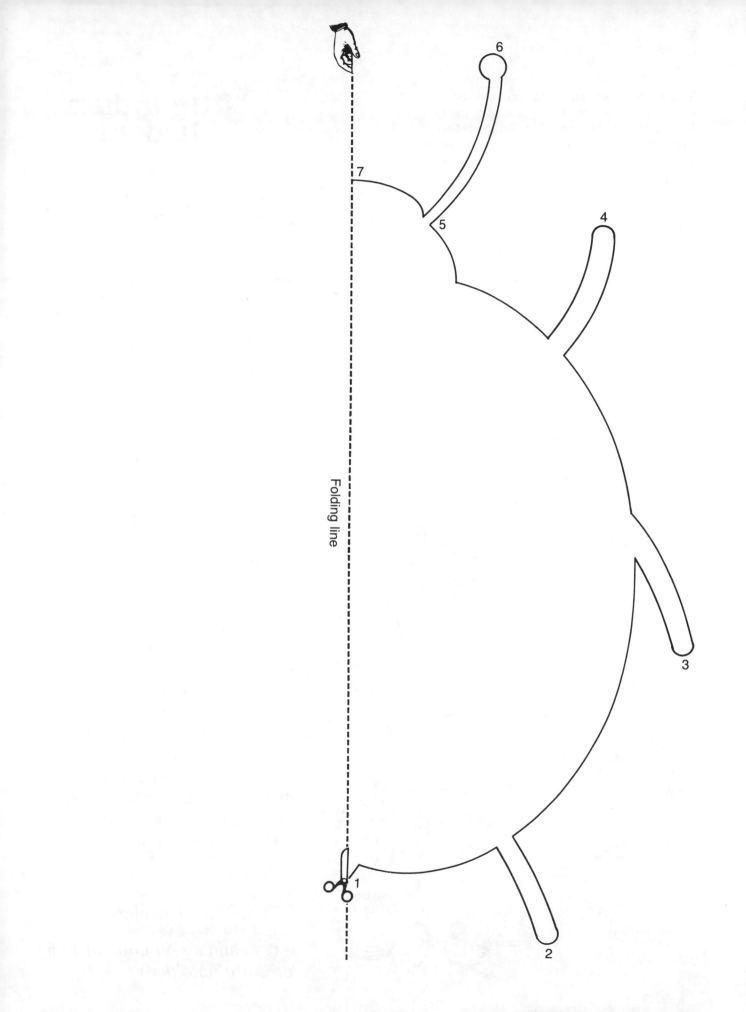

Folding line

You will need scissors and two strips of 6″ × 20″ tissue paper or newspaper. Fold the two strips together into 2″ accordion pleats. Trace the cutting line from the pattern. Cut along the line while you tell the story. Make sure you don't cut the folds. Cut the fringe lines in feathers and skirts.

Little Indian Maidens

One day Chief Eagle Feather went to the village where old Chief Bear Foot lived. This was his first visit.

Eagle Feather asked, "How many sons do you have?"

"Four sons," replied Bear Foot.

"How many daughters do you have?" asked Eagle Feather.

"Many daughters," answered Bear Foot.

"Do you have four daughters?" Eagle Feather asked.

Bear Foot shook his head. "Many daughters," he said proudly.

"Are there five daughters?" asked Eagle Feather.

Again Bear Foot shook his head. "Many daughters," he said.

"Do you have six? Seven? How many daughters?"

Old Chief Bear Foot smiled and said, "Soon you will see." He called to his daughters. They came, one at a time, and stood before their father. Chief Bear Foot presented his daughters to Chief Eagle Feather and counted them. He had (*encourage the group to count with you*):

One fine daughter
   (*unfold one figure*),
Two fine daughters
   (*unfold second figure*),
Three fine daughters
   (*unfold third figure*),
(*. . . and so on until all 10 figures are unfolded*).

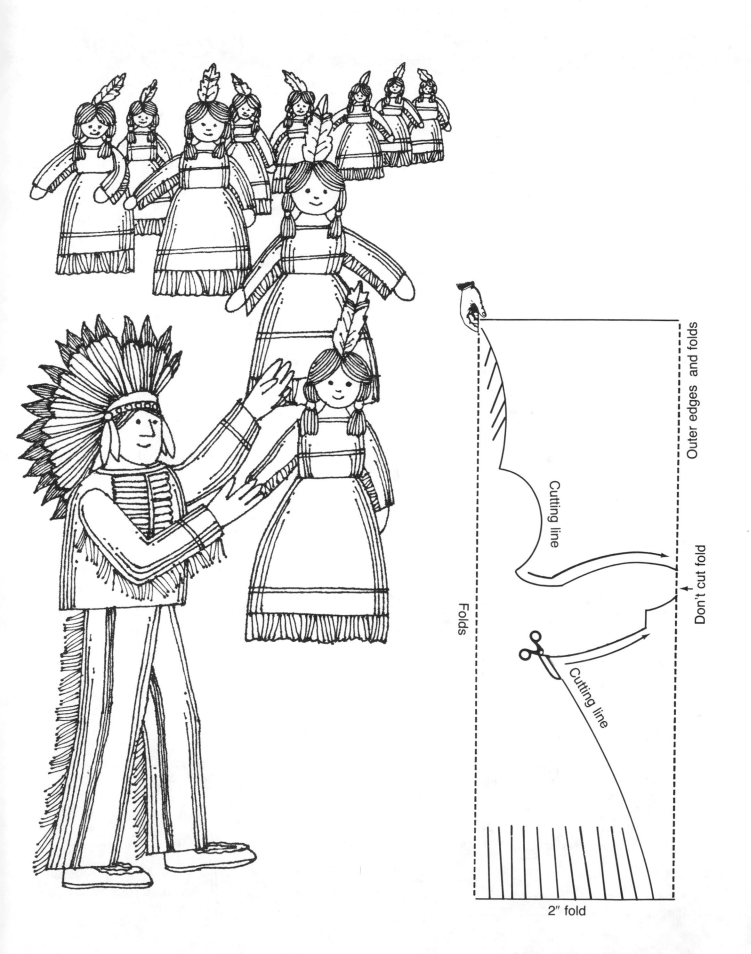

Outer edges and folds

Cutting line

Don't cut fold

Cutting line

Folds

2" fold

You will need scissors and one 8½″ × 10″ sheet of white paper. Use the flat sides of crayons to color one strip green, one red, and one orange. (See the pattern.) Fold the paper into 1¼″ accordion pleats. Trace the cutting line from the pattern.

Mistress Mary

(*Cut along cutting line in orange area while reciting the following:*)

Mistress Mary, quite contrary,
How does your garden grow?
No silver bells, no cockleshells,
Just pretty, orange pumpkins in a row.

(*Cut along cutting line in red area while reciting the following:*)

Mistress Mary, quite contrary,
How does your garden grow?
No silver bells, no cockleshells,
Just pretty, red tulips in a row.

(*Cut along cutting line in green area while reciting the following:*)

Mistress Mary, quite contrary,
How does your garden grow?
No silver bells, no cockleshells,
Just pretty, green trees in a row.
(*Unfold the paper.*)

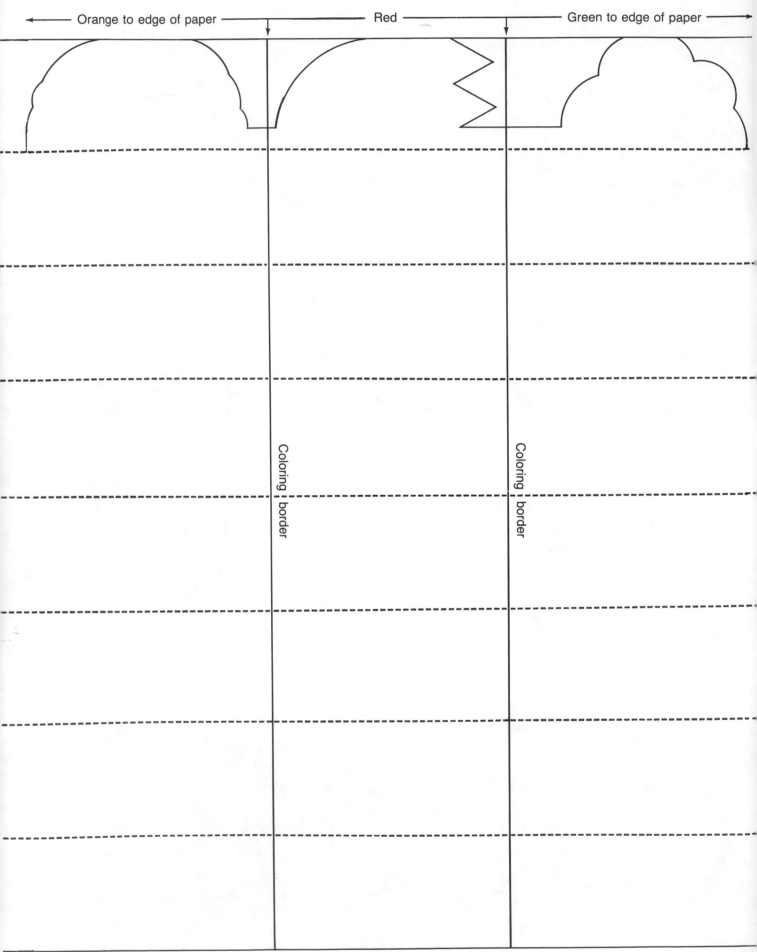

Coloring border

Coloring border

Rain, Rain, Rain

You will need scissors and one 8½″ × 11″ sheet of paper, any color. Trace the folding and cutting lines from the pattern. Fold the paper on the folding line.

Raindrops on the hilltop,
Raindrops on the sea.
Raindrops on the green grass,
But no rain on me.

*(Cut from 1 to 2 along cutting
line while reading or reciting
the poem.)*

*(Repeat the poem while cutting
from 2 to 3. Encourage the
group to say the poem with
you.)*

*(Cut from 3 to 4, repeating the
poem again with the group.)*

Why not? Because I have
(*unfold*) an umbrella!

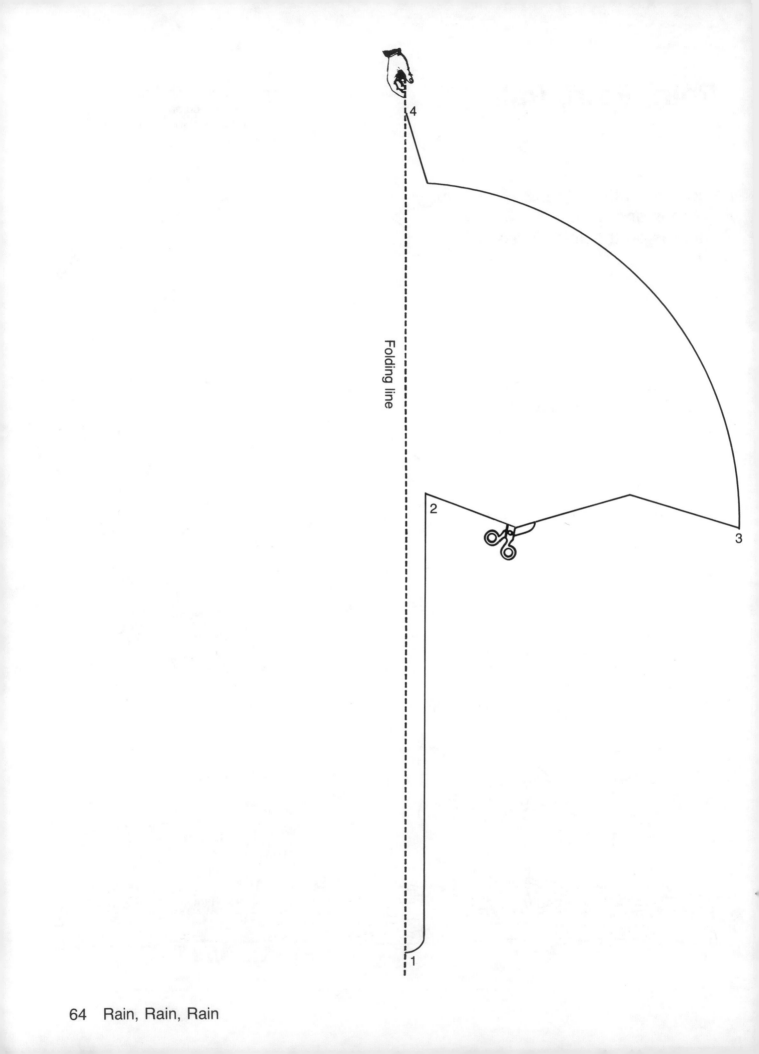

Folding line

4

2

3

1

Part 4

EVERYDAY STORIES

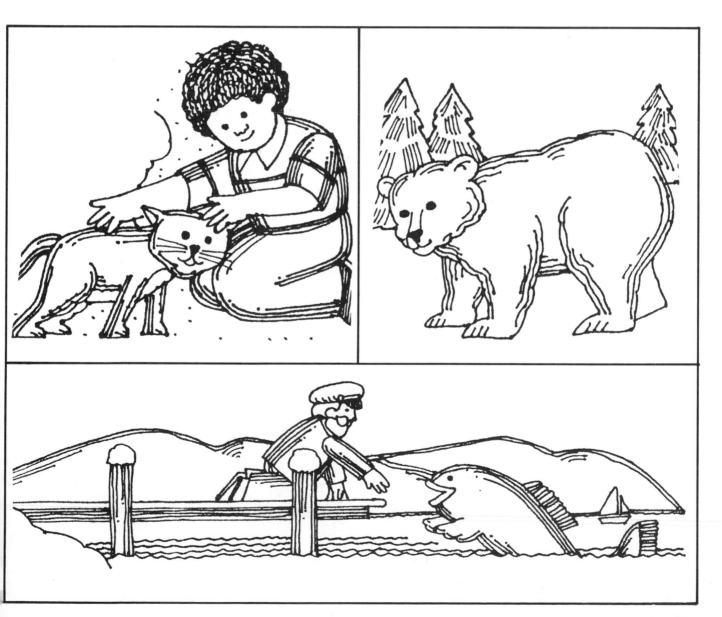

You will need two 8″ × 10″ sheets of paper. Trace the folding lines from the two patterns. While you read the story, fold the paper and display the shapes.

I'd Like to Be . . .

I'm just a piece of paper,
Long and flat.
But I can change quickly,
Just like that!
(*Stamp your foot.*)
I'd like to be a square.
　And the paper became a square.
　　(*Fold on line A.*)

I'm just a piece of paper,
Square and flat.
But I can change quickly,
Just like that!
(*Stamp your foot.*)
I'd like to be a triangle.
　And the paper became a triangle.
　　(*Fold on line B.*)

I'm just a piece of paper,
Pointed and flat.
But I can change quickly
Just like that!
(*Stamp your foot.*)
I'd like to be a diamond.
　And the paper became a diamond.
　　(*Completely unfold paper. Refold on lines C, D, E, and F.*)

I'm just a piece of paper,
Long and flat.
But I can change quickly,
Just like that!
(*Stamp your foot.*)

I'd like to be an ice cream cone.

   And the paper became an ice cream cone.

> *(Completely unfold paper. Refold on lines G and H.)*

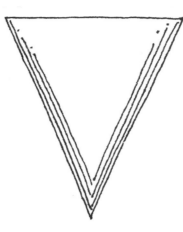

I'm just a piece of paper,
Narrow and flat.
But I can change quickly,
Just like that!
(*Stamp your foot.*)
I'd like to be a hat.

   And the paper became a hat.

> *(Take the second piece of paper. Fold on line I. Then fold on lines J and K, turning both corners back. Then fold on line L, turning top layer of paper up. Flip hat over and fold on line M, turning paper up.)*

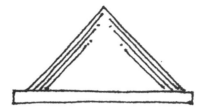

I'm just a piece of paper,
A funny-shaped hat.
But I can change quickly,
Just like that!
(*Stamp your foot.*)
I'd like to be a fan.

   And the paper became a fan.

> *(Completely unfold paper. Starting on line N, accordion pleat the paper into ¾" folds. Hold pleated paper vertically, bend up ¾" from the bottom, and fan out the pleats.)*

Now take a piece of paper,
Long and flat.
(*Unfold paper completely.*)
Can you change it quickly,
Just like that?
(*Stamp your foot.*)

> *(Give a sheet of paper to each child. Have them free-fold the paper into various shapes. You can also give directions for creating some of the shapes from the story.)*

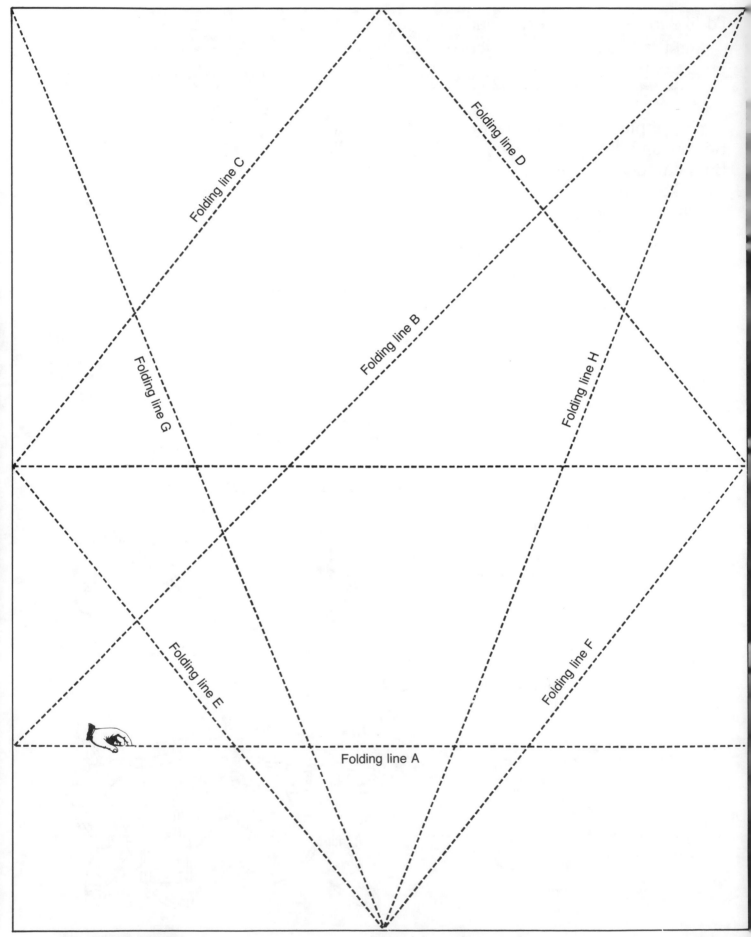

Folding line C

Folding line D

Folding line B

Folding line G

Folding line H

Folding line E

Folding line F

Folding line A

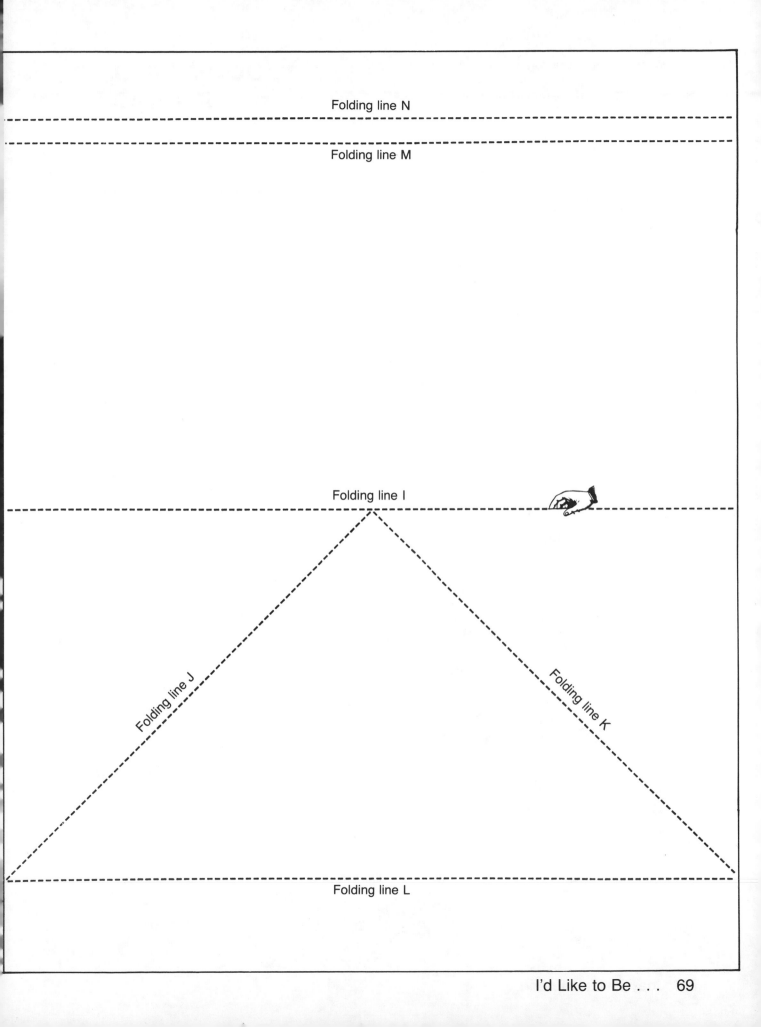

Folding line N

Folding line M

Folding line I

Folding line J

Folding line K

Folding line L

You will need sharp scissors and one 8½″ × 11″ sheet of black paper. Trace the folding and cutting lines from the pattern. Fold the paper along the folding line.

Joey Finds a Friend

Joey and his parents moved to the country. Joey's father built their house on a high hill. (*Cut along the lines from 1 to 2 and from 3 to 4.*)

It had two chimneys. (*Cut along the lines from 4 to 5, from 6 to 7, and from 8 to 9; don't cut the folds between 5 to 6 or 7 to 8.*)

It had two windows. (*Cut out the two Xs.*)

And it had a door. (*Cut out the Y.*)

Joey liked the new house, but he was lonesome. He walked around and around the house. "Mom," he said, "I wish I had someone to play with."

"Maybe someone lives down the road," said his mother.

Joey walked to the end of the road. (*Cut along the lines from 10 to 11.*) But he didn't find anyone there.

He slid down the side of the nearby hill. (*Cut from 12 to 13.*) He didn't find anyone there either.

Joey decided to climb up the other side of the hill. (*Cut from 13 to 14.*)

"Maybe I should go this way," thought Joey. He walked and walked. (*Cut from 14 to 15.*) It was getting dark, and Joey was tired. He decided to sit down and rest. Then he heard something in the bushes behind him.

"It must be a monster," thought Joey. He got up and walked quickly up the long trail. (*Cut from 16 to 17.*)

Joey skipped across the bridge. (*Cut from 17 to 18.*) He said, "I can see that thing moving in the shadows." He heard footsteps, and he saw something crossing over the bridge.

Joey turned and ran down a narrow path. (*Cut from 18 to 19.*) He fell. Then Joey heard a scary sound. "It's getting closer," he thought.

Joey got up and started toward the house. He ran faster and faster. (*Cut from 20 to 21.*)

He stopped before he reached the door. (*Cut from 21 to 22.*)

Joey turned and looked behind him. (*Cut from 23 to 24 and from 25 to 26.*)

"Oh," he said. "It is only a little black kitten that followed me home!" (*Stand cat up by separating folded piece.*)

"Now I have a friend, and I won't be lonesome anymore," said Joey.

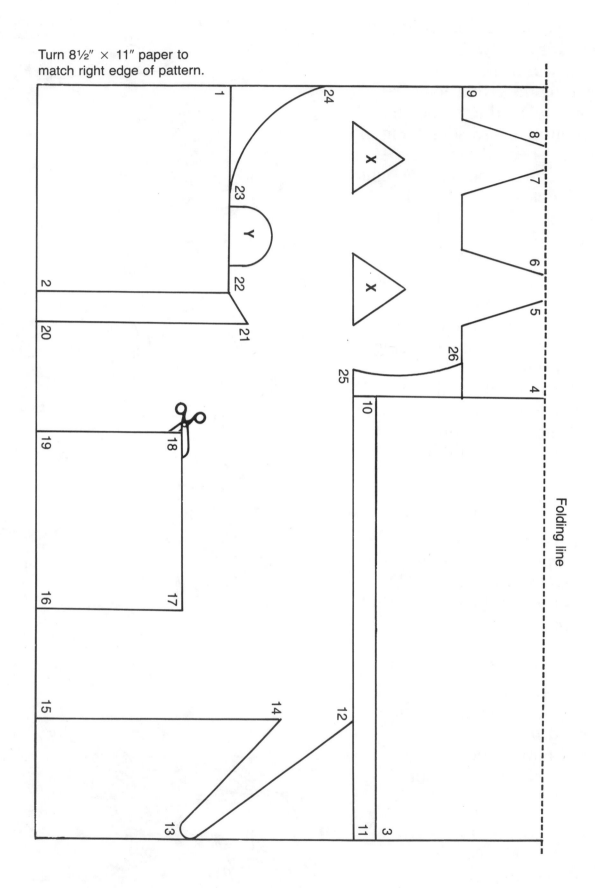

Turn 8½″ × 11″ paper to match right edge of pattern.

Folding line

Too Many Wishes

You will need sharp scissors and one 8½" × 11" sheet of paper. Trace the folding and cutting lines from the pattern. Fold on line A, turning paper back. Then fold on line B, turning paper back. Then fold on C.

Once there was a little old woman and a little old man who lived on the side of a hill. Their house had no doors or windows. (*Cut on line 1.*) They had to climb up and crawl through an opening near the top. (*Cut on line 2.*) They were very poor and did not have much food to eat. (*Hold up paper house.*)

One day the little old man went fishing in the sea. He caught a huge fish. The old man had never seen such a fish. "This will give us food for many days," he said.

"Throw me back in the sea," said the fish, "and I will grant you a wish."

The old man said, "I wish we had a nice house with windows and a door."

"Go home," said the fish.

The old man threw the fish back in the sea and went home. He told his wife what had happened. That night, while they were sleeping, the carpenter elves came. They hammered, they sawed, and they painted. (*Cut along lines 3 and 4. Unfold C to cut along line 5 through one thickness of paper. Fold back. Cut out the two Xs, cutting through only one thickness.*) The elves worked all night. (*Unfold at line C, and hold up paper house.*)

The next morning, the old man and the old woman woke up in a nice little house with windows and a door. (*Partly unfold at line B.*)

"This is nice," said the old man.

But the old woman wanted a bigger house. "Go ask the fish for a mansion in the country," she said.

The old man went back to the sea. "Fish, fish," he called. "We want a mansion in the country."

"Go home," said the fish.

That night the carpenter elves came again. (*Unfold at B. Refold on line C.*) They hammered, they sawed, and they painted. (*Cut on line 6; cut out Z; cut out Y through only one thickness of paper.*) The elves worked all night. (*Unfold at C, partly unfold at A, and hold up house.*)

The next morning, the old woman and the old man woke up in a beautiful mansion in the country. "Oh, this is very nice," said the old woman. "But I want a bigger house. Go ask the fish for a palace fit for a king and queen."

The old man went back to the sea. "Fish, fish," he called. "We want a palace fit for a king and queen."

"Go home," said the fish.

That night the carpenter elves came again. (*Unfold at A. Refold on line C.*) They hammered, they sawed, and they painted. (*Cut on lines 7 and 8 to dot.*) The elves worked all night. (*Unfold at C, fold doors open, and hold up house.*)

The next morning, the old woman and the old man woke up in a palace fit for a king and queen. "I have never seen anything like this before," said the old woman. "But I want a bigger house."

"No," said the old man. "This is enough."

"Just one more," said the old woman. "Go ask the fish for a castle with a tower that will reach to the sky."

The old man went back to the sea. "Fish, fish," he called. "We want a castle with a tower that will reach to the sky."

"Go home," said the fish.

The old woman and the old man went to bed. The next morning, they woke up to find themselves back in their home on the side of a hill. (*Unfold doors. Refold paper on lines B and C.*) And there they are living until this day.

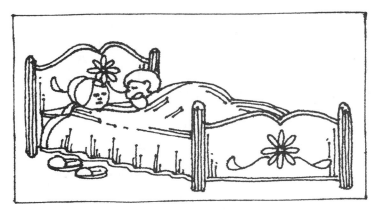

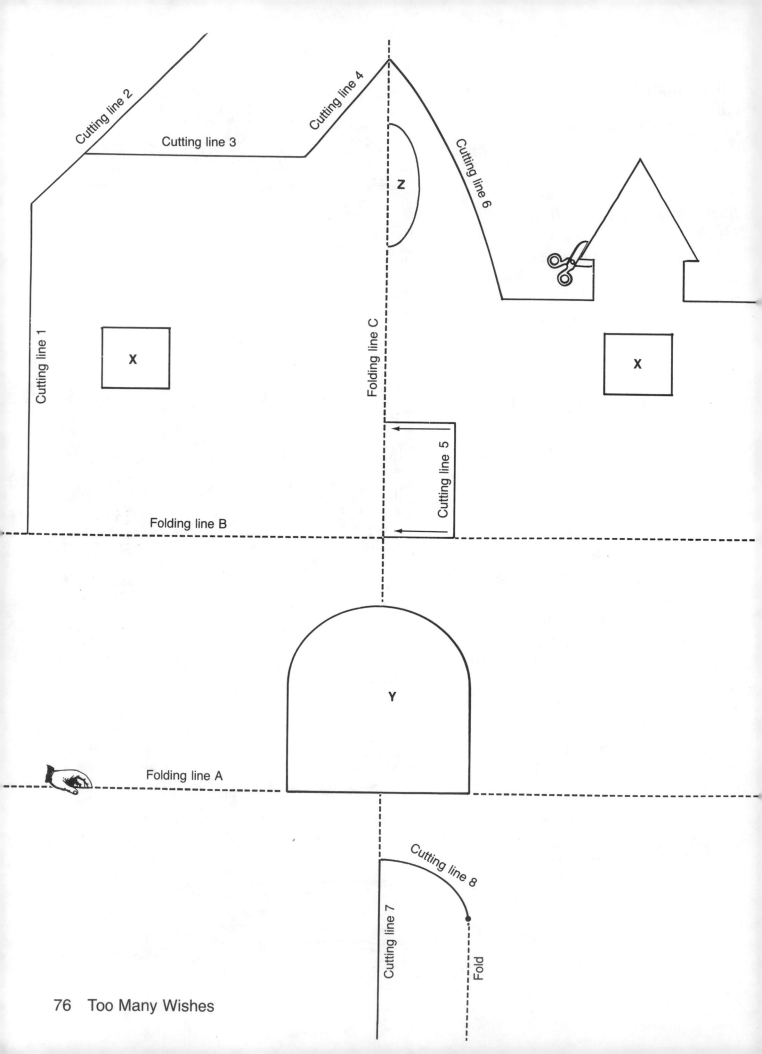

Cutting line 2

Cutting line 3

Cutting line 4

Cutting line 6

Z

Cutting line 1

X

Folding line C

X

Cutting line 5

Folding line B

Y

Folding line A

Cutting line 8

Cutting line 7

Fold

Two Scared Mice

You will need sharp scissors and one 8½″ × 11″ sheet of paper. Fold the paper on the folding line and trace the cutting lines from the pattern.

Very early one morning, while it was still dark, two little mice peeked out of a hole in the barn.

"I think it's clear. Let's go!" said Big Mouse. "I'm hungry."

"Be careful," said Little Mouse. The two mice crawled slowly out onto the barn floor. (*Cut from 1 to 2.*)

They crept around an old barrel. (*Cut from 2 to 3.*)

Together they scampered over to the corn bin. (*Cut from 3 to 4.*)

Suddenly the mice heard a strange sound. They couldn't run back to the hole, because something was standing in front of it. They ran along the edge of the barn floor. (*Cut from 4 to 5.*)

"It must be one of the barn animals," said Little Mouse.

"No, I don't think so," Big Mouse said. They stopped at the corner. (*Cut from 5 to 6.*)

"It's coming after us," said Big Mouse. "Quick, jump into the box." (*Cut out the area marked by the X.*) And they did. A plump hand with strong fingers reached into the box and just missed the two mice. They soon found their way out of the box. (*Cut from 6 to 7.*) The morning sun began to rise, and it cast light into the barn.

As the mice stopped to rest, a large shadow fell over them. They ran around in circles, terrified. (*Cut from 7 to 8.*)

They raced to the top of a hay pile. There they found a safe place to hide. (*Cut from 8 to 9.*)

"We will wait here until that thing is gone," Little Mouse said.

"Yes," said Big Mouse, "then we can go back to the corn bin and eat our breakfast."

The two mice stayed in their hiding place. They listened to the heavy sound of large feet moving out of the barn. Who was in the barn? (*Unfold the paper.*) It was only the farmer's wife, who had come to gather the eggs.

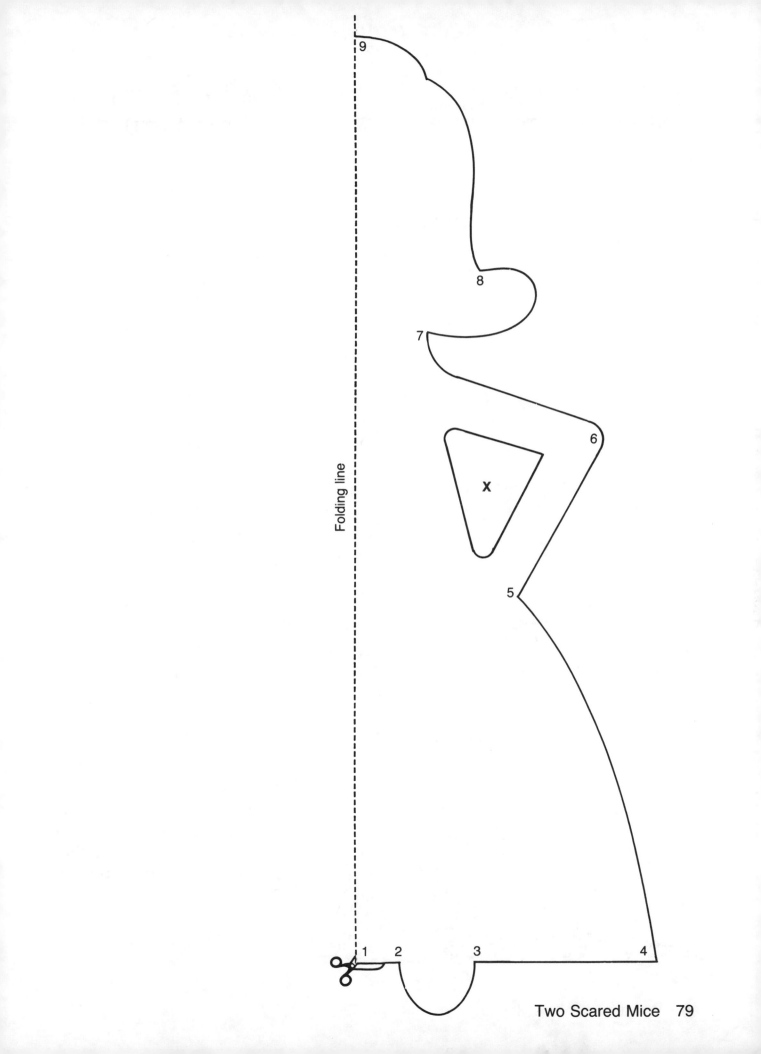

Folding line

X

1 2 3 4

5

6

7

8

9

Two Scared Mice 79

You will need scissors and one 8½″ × 11″ sheet of paper. Fold the paper and trace the cutting lines from the pattern.

Who Lives in This House?

There is a very special house,
In a very special forest,
Outside a very special town.
It belongs to someone with very special ears. (*Cut on line 1; unfold the paper*).

Could it be an elephant with ears like this? No, but elephants do have special ears. They have the largest ears in the world.

There is a very special house,
In a very special forest,
Outside a very special town.
And it belongs to someone with very special ears. (*Cut on line 2; unfold.*)

Could it be a rabbit with ears like this? No, but rabbits do have special ears. They can make their ears stand up straight or lay down on their backs.

There is a very special house,
In a very special forest,
Outside a very special town.
And it belongs to someone with very special ears. (*Cut on line 3: unfold.*)

Could it be a deer with tiny horns and ears like this? No, but deer do have special ears that help them hear the sounds in the forest.

There is a very special house,
In a very special forest,
Outside a very special town.
And it belongs to someone with very special ears. (*Cut on line 4; unfold.*)

Could it be a bear with small, small ears? No, but bears do have special ears that are just right for them.

Who could live in this very special house,
In a very special forest,
Outside a very special town?
(*Cut on line 5; unfold.*)

It belongs to a person with special ears—just like yours!

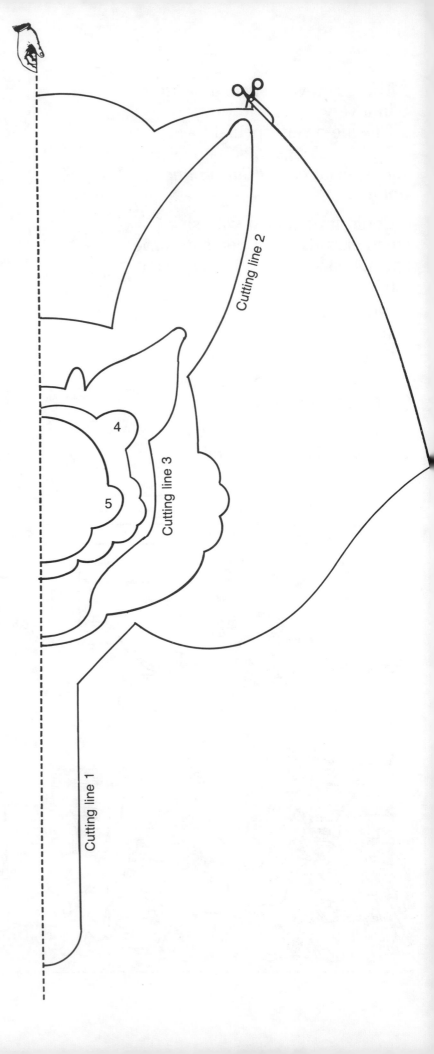

Cutting line 2

Cutting line 3

4

5

Cutting line 1

Part 5

SPECIAL PAPER STORIES

A Clown's Best Trick

You will need scissors, two 3″ × 5″ cards, one 4″ × 6″ card, and one 4″ × 12″ piece of tagboard.

Four clowns were sitting around with nothing to do. They decided to have a contest to see who could perform the best paper trick.

Red Clown said, "I can take this piece of paper (*3″ × 5″ card*), make a few cuts, and I will have a bracelet." (*Fold card across to make 3″ × 2½″ shape.*)

The other clowns laughed. "You can't do that," they said.

After a few cuts (*cut according to pattern shown below*), Red Clown put on his bracelet.

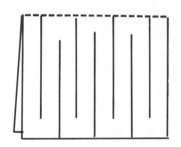

Green Clown said, "I can take this piece of paper (*3″ × 5″ card*), make a few cuts, and I will have a necklace." (*Fold card lengthwise to make 1½″ × 5″ shape.*)

The other clowns laughed. "You can't do that," they said.

After a few cuts (*cut according to pattern shown below*), Green Clown put on her necklace.

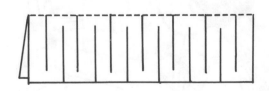

Blue Clown said, "I can take this piece of paper (*4" × 6" card*), make a few cuts, and I will have a belt." (*Fold card lengthwise to make 2" × 6" shape.*)

The other clowns laughed. "You can't do that," they said.

After a few cuts (*cut according to pattern shown below*), Blue Clown put on his belt.

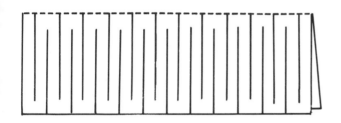

Orange Clown didn't say anything. The other clowns did not laugh. She took a piece of paper (*fold the 4" x 12" tagboard lengthwise*) and started cutting. (*Cut according to pattern shown below.*) Orange Clown made a door. (*Carefully place your feet on the corners of the cutout. Pull the strip up and out to form a large rectangular door.*) The four clowns walked through the door and disappeared.

(After you cut the bracelet, necklace, and belt, you may want to put them on. After you cut the "door," stretch it out to allow the children to crawl through it *carefully*.)

Make partial cuts according to the patterns. Open each card and cut across the fold, but do not cut the folds on the two end sections. Gently stretch out the cards.

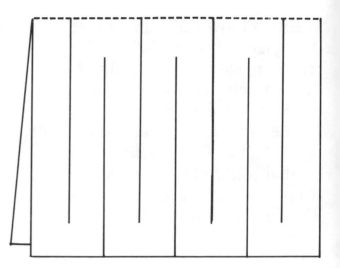

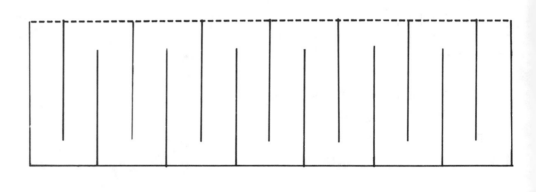

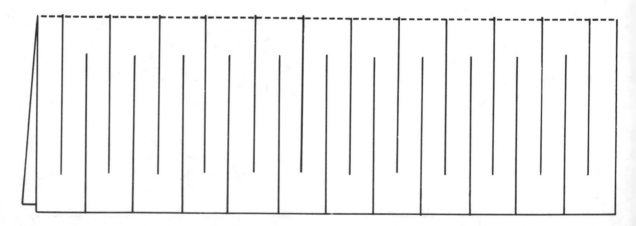

This pattern shown half-size.

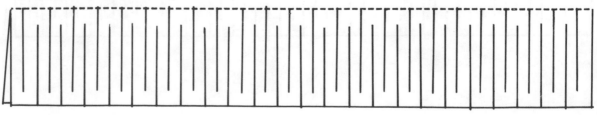

Suzie's Special Seed

Suzie spent the summer in Hawaii visiting Grandpa. One day, Grandpa gave her a big, green seed. "Suzie," he said, "this is a special seed. I want you to plant it before you leave for home."

Suzie planted her special seed near the seashore. Grandpa instructed her to lay the seed on its side and to cover half of it with sand and soil. She marked the spot by piling rocks nearby so she could find it again next summer.

All through the year, Suzie thought about her special seed and wondered if it would grow. She knew it would have plenty of water from the rains.

You will need scissors, a rubber band, and three 8½" × 11" sheets of green construction paper. Lay one sheet of paper on a flat surface. Begin rolling the paper to make a roll 8½" long. Roll loosely until three inches are left. Lay the second sheet on top and continue rolling to the last three inches. Lay the third sheet on top and roll it up. Place a rubber band loosely around the bottom half of the roll.

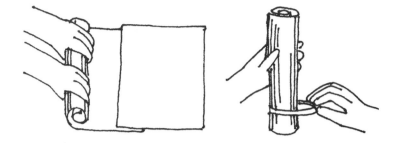

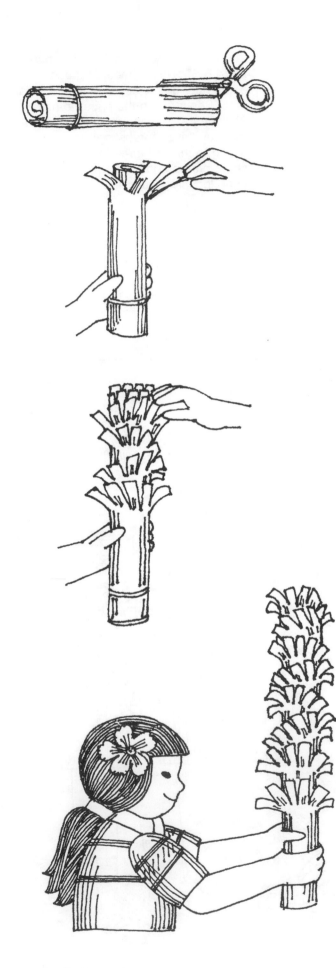

The following summer when she visited Grandpa, Suzie ran to the pile of rocks. (*Starting at the top of the roll of paper, make 1" cuts, cutting down 2½".*) Her seed was growing! It had a trunk and a few small leaves at the top. (*Bend out 3 leaves.*)

The next year when she returned to Hawaii, the tree was as tall as Suzie was, and it was growing nicely. (*Pull paper carefully from the inside center; bend out leaves.*)

Every year she watched her tree grow. After four years, the tree was higher than Grandpa's house. (*Pull up a little more paper from the center; bend out a few more leaves.*)

Again, the next year on her visit, Suzie checked her tree and saw that it had grown even taller. (*Pull a little more paper from the center, and bend out the remaining leaves.*)

Grandpa asked, "Remember the special seed that I gave you? It had a green husk on the outside, but inside was a black coconut seed. Your tree is a coconut palm."

"Will it have coconuts?" asked Suzie.

"Yes," said Grandpa, "but it will take six or seven years."

"How many coconuts will it have?" she asked.

"Some trees will grow a hundred coconuts a year. But the tree will have only a few the first time."

Vacation was over, and it was time for Suzie to go home. She thanked Grandpa for that special seed. "Maybe next year," thought Suzie, "my tree will have coconuts."

You will need scissors and one piece of newspaper, about 24″ × 14″. Fold the newspaper to 12″ × 14″. Then fold it again to 12″ × 7″.

The Merry-Go, Merry-Go-Round

A little girl went to the park to play. She played on the swings awhile. Then she played on the teeter-totter awhile. Then she slid down the slide. Then she saw something else on the playground.

"This looks like fun," she said. And she climbed on it. (*Begin folding the paper according to the pattern. Then trace the cutting lines from the pattern.*)

"May I join you?" asked another little girl.

"Come on," said the first girl.

"Can I play too?" asked a third girl.

"Let me push," said a fourth girl.

"Wait for me," called a fifth girl. (*Begin cutting along the cutting lines.*)

"It's my turn," said a sixth girl.

Soon there were eight little girls who were riding, playing, and laughing in the park. What were they playing on? (*Unfold the paper; set it on a flat surface. Spin the cutout around.*)

Around and around went the merry-go, merry-go, merry-go-round.

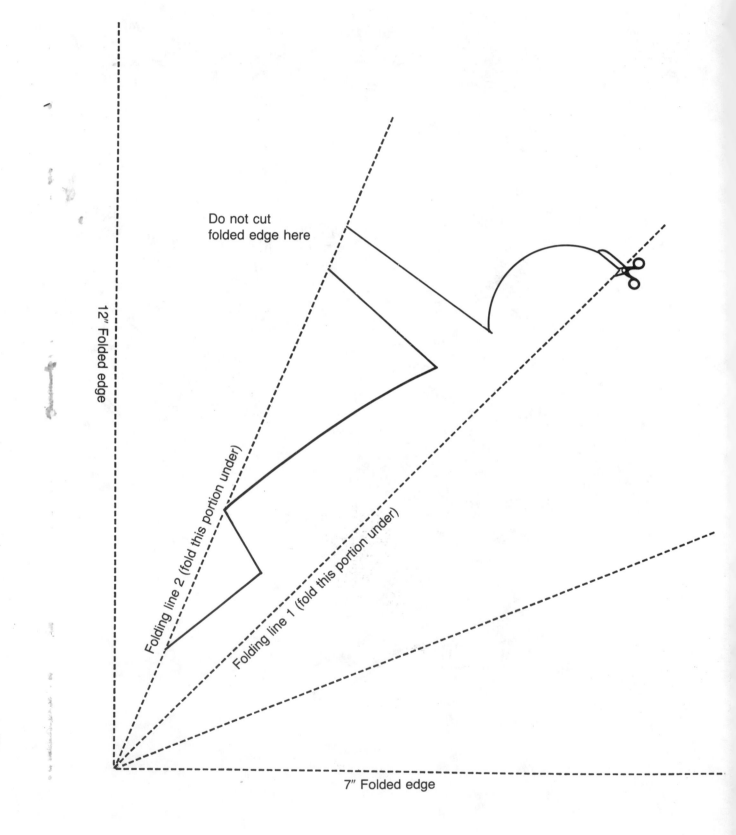

Do not cut
folded edge here

12" Folded edge

Folding line 2 (fold this portion under)

Folding line 1 (fold this portion under)

7" Folded edge